Baltimore Chronicles
Volume 1

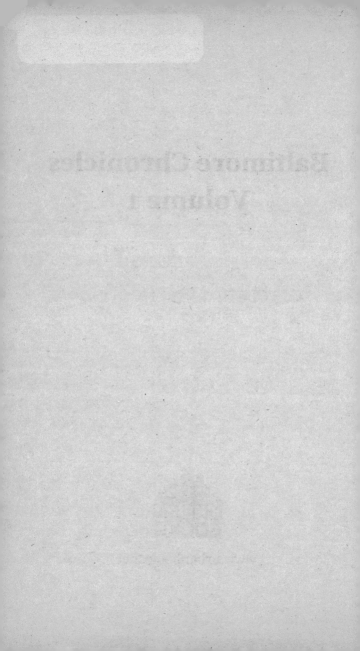

Baltimore Chronicles
Volume 1

Treasure Hernandez

URBAN
BOOKS

www.urbanbooks.net

Urban Books, LLC
78 East Industry Court
Deer Park, NY 11729

ISBN 13: 978-1-60162-495-6
ISBN 10: 1-60162-495-6

First Mass Paperback Printing January 2012
First Trade Paperback Printing September 2010
Printed in the United States of America

10 9 8 7 6 5 4 3 2 1

Distributed by Kensington Publishing Corp.
Submit Wholesale Orders to:
Kensington Publishing Corp.
C/O Penguin Group (USA) Inc.
Attention: Order Processing
405 Murray Hill Parkway
East Rutherford, NJ 07073-2316
Phone: 1-800-526-0275
Fax: 1-800-227-9604

Chapter 1

The Take Down

Detective Derek Fuller splashed water on his face, took a deep breath, and looked up at himself in the small, dull mirror that hung in the men's bathroom inside the station house. He noticed the bags that were starting to form under his eyes, but he knew those came with the territory. Fighting against the Maryland drug trade was not an easy win. Shaking off his jitters, Derek stared at himself. He thought that despite those bags, his smooth cinnamon-colored skin and chestnut brown eyes still made him a fine-ass dude.

Refocusing, Derek spoke to himself. "Let's get it, nigga. This ain't no time to have second thoughts." He checked his gear, shifted his bulletproof vest, and shrugged into his raid jacket. It was six o'clock in the morning, and he had to get into the right state of mind for the task at hand. Walking back out into the squad room, he put on his game face.

"I hope everybody is ready for Scar. Let's fuckin' roll and take this nigga out. This mu'fucka only thinks he's the leader of the bitch-ass Dirty Money Crew," Derek announced to the four officers who comprised his unit. They all stood at attention and started gathering their battle gear.

"Yo, Fuller, can I bring this baby with me?" Officer Rodriguez asked, picking up the brand new MP-5 they had just acquired. The big weapon looked out of place in the petite woman's hands. To the average eye, she would appear weak and out of her element, but Fuller had come up in the academy with Rodriguez and knew never to underestimate her. She had the gumption that most men never mustered, and she was an asset to his team. He trusted Rodriguez with his life, and in the game they played, that meant a lot. She never hesitated to pull a trigger, and if he was the first man through the door, she was always right behind him.

"Damn straight," Derek replied, flashing his perfect smile and leading his unit out the door.

Derek felt powerful in his new position as a lead detective with the Baltimore Narcotics

Unit of the Maryland State Police. Living and working in the roughest part of Baltimore, Derek had put in work, moving up from a car-chasing, ticket-giving state trooper to a narcotics street officer, and now leader of his own narcotics interdiction unit. Derek's unit was charged with taking down the so-called Dirty Money Crew and their notorious leader, Stephon "Scar" Johnson.

Everyone in the Baltimore area knew about Scar and his powerful drug ring. He ran cocaine up and down the interstate with ease. On top of that, he was a jack of all trades. He had his hand in everything from extortion and illegal gambling to prostitution. If there was money to be made in the underworld of B-more, then Scar was getting it. Scar had been reigning terror on the streets for years now. He was considered the Rayful Edmond of Baltimore; only difference was he didn't get caught. He deemed himself untouchable and moved like a ghost through the streets, getting money but going unseen most of the time. Rumor had it that on his climb to the top, Scar had taken out ten police officers and two government officials; but with no proof and witnesses who always turned up dead or missing, it had been an almost impossible undertaking for the overmatched and undermanned state troopers to touch Scar.

That did not stop Derek's unit from pursuing Scar. Derek was aware of what he needed to do to prove himself to his bosses and the crime syndicates in the streets. His success as a detective depended on the attention he would receive for taking Scar down.

As Derek and his unit arrived at their destination in the worst hood in Baltimore, Derek shook his head and smiled. It was just like the confidential informant had told the unit; Scar was making a very rare early morning creep appearance at one of his most lucrative trap houses. When Derek noticed Scar's tricked-out black Escalade, complete with its candy paint job, parked on the side of the trap house, Derek felt his dick jump in his pants. He was that excited by this opportunity to shine.

"Here we fuckin' go!" Derek mumbled under his breath, geeking himself up for the task at hand. His heart was beating so fast that it threatened to jump out of his chest. He turned to Cassell and asked, "You got the warrant?"

"Signed, sealed, and delivered," Cassell replied, revealing an edge of the warrant from out of his breast pocket.

Some would say he was being overcautious with the warrant, but Derek wasn't about to make the same mistake twice. A few years back, due to his recklessness, he had busted a local drug dealer without a warrant. Needless to say, the drug dealer was set free. That incident didn't help his reputation within the police force, and he had worked hard to gain back respect.

Satisfied that everything was in order just how he'd planned it, Derek was ready for the raid. Yanking his Glock out of his hip holster, Derek barely put his vehicle in park before he swung the door open and jumped out. He waved his hands over his head, placed his fingers up to his lips, and made a fist, signaling his unit to get into their rehearsed raid positions.

They all silently exited their black Impalas. Ducking low, they fell in line one behind the other and stacked on the door. Derek was first in the stack; he would announce their arrival. The ram holder stood on the opposite side of the door, and the rest of the unit knew their roles in bringing up the back of the stack. Derek raised his right hand and silently counted down. *Three, two, one.*

At that, the ram holder sent the heavy duty metal crashing into the shabby plywood door. The wood splintered open with one hit. Inside, bodies began scrambling in all directions.

"Police! Police! Put ya fuckin' hands up now!" Derek screamed, waving his weapon back and forth, pointing it at all of Scar's scrambling workers for emphasis. All of the members of the unit trampled inside, grabbing whomever they could and tossing them to the ground.

Derek continued into the house with his gun drawn, keeping his back close to the walls. He had his eye on the prize, and he was not going to stop until he had it in custody. Derek came to a closed door at the back of the house. With his gun trained on the door, he kicked it open.

"Damn, man, put the gun down. You ain't gotta go all hard and shit," Scar said calmly as he exhaled a cigar smoke ring in front of him, poisoning the air surrounding him.

Derek shook his head. He needed this take down to be as dramatic as possible, and Scar's laid-back attitude wasn't helping.

"Put your fucking hands up, mu'fucka!" Derek screamed, pointing his gun right at Scar's head. "Now! Show me your hands!"

"A'ight, a'ight. Calm down, cowboy," Scar said, smirking and stubbing out his cigar on the table he sat behind.

Derek was getting more pissed by the minute. He didn't want to look like a punk in front of his unit, while Scar was looking cool, calm, and collected.

"They pay you to act all extra?" Scar asked, still smiling.

"Let's go! Stand the fuck up, nigga!" Derek barked again.

"I got one better for you. I will put my hands out so you can cuff me." Scar chuckled, his smile causing his severely disfigured charcoal-colored face to contort into a monstrous mug. Pushing away from the table, Scar lifted his six foot three inch gorilla frame up from the chair. Laughing like he had heard a joke, Scar turned around and assumed the handcuffing position.

"Cuff this son of a bitch!" Derek spat as one of his officers moved in swiftly to lock the cuffs on Scar's thick wrists.

"Son of a bitch? Ain't that the pot calling the kettle black?" Scar replied, still laughing.

Derek grabbed the cuffs roughly, making sure they were clamped extra tight so the metal would cut into Scar's skin and shut him up. That would teach him not to play games.

There were just some things that shouldn't be said in front of the members of the unit. No need to arouse anyone's suspicions.

Derek led Scar out of the house, and just like he had planned, the media trucks and cameras were right on time to get coverage of the raid.

"Detective Fuller, how did you do this so smoothly when no other law enforcement units could take down the notorious Stephon 'Scar' Johnson?" a female reporter yelled out as Derek rushed passed her with Scar in tow.

"It was all in a day's work," Derek wolfed out as he pushed Scar's head down into the back of the police car.

Derek looked and felt like a hero. He had taken down the big, bad drug kingpin. He could not contain his proud smile. He was the man.

Derek and his unit pulled into the prisoner drop-off area in the back of the station house and unloaded Scar and some of his crew.

"Ay, man, when all the pomp and circumstance is done, maybe we can break bread, you know, have a drink and shit," Scar said, smiling at Derek mischievously.

"Nah, buddy. You'll be breaking bread with your fellow inmates soon enough," Derek said smoothly, slapping five with some of his unit members and walking away, leaving Scar to be processed.

Derek continued to crack jokes with his unit as they proceeded to the front of the station house. Pushing open the door, they were surprised by the way they were greeted. It was like the other officers and staff at the station house had planned a surprise party. They all stopped to turn and see the unit enter, and they were cheering and whistling loudly.

Derek could not contain his pride. He loved the attention, especially when he noticed Chief William Scott standing in front of the uproarious crowd. The chief stepped forward, placing his hands up to quiet the cheers so he could speak. He loved to hear himself speak.

"Here they are, the untouchable Baltimore Narcotics Unit. They have done in one day what every other law enforcement agency in Maryland and the feds have tried to do for years. Led by one of the finest detectives in state trooper history, Derek Fuller," Chief Scott announced, placing one hand on Derek's shoulder and grabbing his other hand for a firm handshake. The crowd of state troopers and administrative staff erupted in cheers again.

Derek bowed his head slightly, trying to act modest, but he loved the attention. He basked in it. It was what he had waited so long for, to be considered great.

He returned the chief's handshake. "I couldn't have done it without the best unit around—Rodriguez, Bolden, Archie, and Cassell. Thank you all for being brave soldiers. This take down was only possible because of the hard work of every member of my team. We have all dedicated countless man hours in the pursuit of justice, and now today is our day," Derek said for good measure. In his head, he was thinking it was all him. Little did they know that he could have singlehandedly taken Scar down, but that was a secret he would have to keep.

"Come down to my office, Detective Fuller. I want to speak to you," Chief Scott leaned into Derek's ear and whispered as the crowd began to break up and surround the other unit members.

Derek's heart jumped in his chest. Everyone knew that it was hard for a black man to get ahead in the Maryland State Police. The fact that this white chief, who was known to be a redneck, wanted to speak to him alone made Derek feel important. It was all working out exactly as he had envisioned it.

He followed the chief downstairs to his office, where Chief Scott offered Derek a seat on his famed leather couch—another rare occurrence. Usually an invitation to Chief Scott's office was only for troopers to get an ass-chewing or disciplinary action taken against them. Derek knew this time would be different.

Chief Scott slid his fat stomach behind his desk, put a finger full of chewing tobacco into his cheek, and looked at Derek seriously. "Detective Fuller. I don't call many people to my office for compliments, but what you did today was beyond remarkable. Taking down one of the biggest bastard drug lords the state of Maryland has ever seen was more than a simple task. Those fucking DEA federal bastards couldn't do it this long with all their corrupt agents and payoffs. You have exceeded any expectations I had ever dreamed of for your unit, and for that, I commend you."

Derek leaned back and smiled. "Thank you, sir."

"Detective Fuller, I truly think you have what it takes to be higher up in the department one day . . . maybe even sit at this desk as chief," Chief Scott said seriously, spitting his gooey, chewed-up tobacco into a can on his desk.

Derek was glowing from the accolades he was receiving. "Well, Chief, I appreciate the compliment. I just want to work hard and continue to make you and the department proud. It took months of surveillance and lots of footwork on the streets," he said, continuing the act he'd been performing all day, "but at the end of the day, that bastard Scar Johnson deserved to go down. I'm just glad it's over." Derek stood up from the couch. "Now, after I finish the paperwork, I'm going home to my family, who I have neglected for the last six months. I'm sure my wife will be happy to see me," Derek said. Just thinking about his beautiful woman made him smile again.

"I've seen your wife. I would be on my way home too," Chief Scott commented with a smile, sending Derek on his way.

Derek turned his key in the door to his modest single-family home, and he could already smell the aroma of his dinner wafting through the house. He loved his wife so much. She was a triple threat—a good mother, a working professional, and a damned good wife. "Hello?" Derek called out and then waited.

"Daddy! Daddy!" he heard his kids screaming as they ran toward him at top speed. They were not used to him being home at night. Most of the time, he would come in after a long stakeout and they would already be asleep, so his presence was a welcome surprise.

"Ay, baby girl and my big man," Derek sang, picking up his two-year-old daughter and rubbing his six-year-old son's head.

"We saw you on the news today!" his son announced proudly, holding onto his father like he never wanted him to leave again.

With kids hanging onto him, Derek moved slowly toward the kitchen, where he knew Tiphani waited for him. Just like he expected, his sexy wife stood by the stove with her back turned, her long jet-black hair lying on her back and her apple bottom looking perfect in her fitted jeans.

Derek put his daughter down and grabbed his wife around her waist from the back. He inhaled the scent of her strawberry shampoo and tucked her hair behind her ear so he could kiss the smooth skin of her neck.

She smiled. "Hey, hey . . . you have to wait for all of that," she sang, putting her stirring spoon down and turning to greet her heroic husband properly.

"Well, hurry up and feed these rugrats so I won't have to wait too long," Derek whispered in her ear. He could feel his nature rising. After almost ten years of marriage, he was still attracted to his wife like they had just begun dating. He never grew tired or bored with her, and it was a plus that she kept herself looking right with regular manicures, pedicures, and facials. In his line of work, divorce was rampant, but Derek and Tiphani had stood the test of time. Derek was grateful to have a partner who understood that sometimes his work had to come first, and he gave her the same respect.

After dinner, Derek tucked the kids into bed while Tiphani cleaned up the dishes. As soon as the little ones drifted off, Derek sneaked back downstairs and watched his wife's sexy frame move around the kitchen. Derek was in awe of her beautiful, flawless caramel skin, her almond-shaped eyes, and beautiful hourglass figure.

He rushed into the kitchen and grabbed her roughly, lifting her off her feet.

"Wait, silly. Let's go upstairs," she said with a giggle.

"I can't wait anymore. Seeing your ass in them jeans got me on rock!" Derek exclaimed, fumbling with the button on her jeans. She acquiesced, throwing her hands around his neck. Derek hoisted her onto their granite countertop and yanked off her jeans, pulling her black lace thong off with them. He inhaled, excited by the sight of her beautifully trimmed triangle. "Fuck . . . you look so damn good! I missed you, baby," he huffed, barely able to contain himself.

Tiphani licked her fingers seductively and rubbed her clitoris, causing it to swell slightly. Derek had finally got his own pants off. His medium-sized member stood at full attention. He was a firm believer that it wasn't the size that mattered; it was what you did with what you had that made all the difference. Derek began licking the inside of her thighs.

"Ahh," Tiphani grunted, throwing her head back. Derek teased around her thighs until she put her hand on his head and forced it between her legs. He stuck his tongue out and licked her clit softly. Tiphani slid her hot box toward his tongue in ecstasy. "I want you," she whispered.

At that, Derek lifted his head, grabbed his dick, and drove it into his wife's soaking wet opening with full force. She let out a short gasp as Derek dug further into her flesh. Tiphani dug her nails into his shoulders. He began to pump harder.

Suddenly, something happened. Derek recoiled slightly. Tiphani closed her legs around his back, trying to keep him inside her. She was hoping that it didn't happen again.

"Urgghhh!" Derek growled, collapsing.

Tiphani slouched her shoulders and lowered her head. He had finished less than two minutes after he had started.

"Fuck!" he cursed himself, his cheeks flaming over with embarrassment. "I'm so sorry, baby. I was just so excited to feel you," Derek said, making excuses for his shortcomings.

"I know you were just excited. That shit was still good, baby," Tiphani consoled as she hugged him.

"Did you at least cum?" Derek asked.

Is he fuckin' kidding me with that question? Tiphani screamed silently in her head. "Hell yeah, baby. You know I cum as soon as you touch me," she lied as she hugged him and hid her face. Derek continued to apologize, and she continued to console him.

This shit is so out of control right now! Tiphani thought as she rolled her eyes behind Derek's back. It wasn't like he came fast and stayed hard where he could please her too. After his nut, he was a goner, leaving her unsatisfied and royally pissed the fuck off.

Derek didn't know if she was telling the truth, but he did know that his premature ejaculation was starting to become a problem.

Chapter 2

Tables Turned

It had been three months since the raid, and the day had finally come. Security was tight as Derek walked up to the courthouse. He could hardly make it to the steps because there were so many reporters and spectators outside. Scar's impending trial had been in the news for weeks. There had even been a countdown of sorts. The media had dubbed it the Trial of the Year. When some of the media hounds noticed Derek, they almost trampled each other to be the first to get a statement from him.

"Detective Fuller, are you nervous to face the notorious Scar Johnson?" a reporter called out, shoving a microphone into Derek's face.

"Are you kidding me with that question? If I wasn't nervous to bring him down in his own hood, why would I be nervous about facing him in a court of law?" Derek replied, giving the reporter a bit of heat. After he set the media straight, Derek smoothed the front of his Brooks Brothers suit and continued his stride up the courthouse steps.

It was no better inside the courtroom. There were throngs of cameras and reporters lined up around the back and sides. Derek sat on the bench directly behind the prosecutor's table and looked around. He could feel more than one pair of icy eyes on him. There were numerous members of Scar's crew peppered throughout the courtroom crowd, and they weren't hiding their glares. Derek didn't care because it just added to the drama of the scene and made him look better.

Derek turned around just in time to see the court officers leading Scar to the defendant's table. Scar had a huge smile plastered on his face, and he stared directly at Derek.

Knowing that all eyes would be on him, Derek frowned at Scar and shook his head. "Ain't this a bitch?" Derek mumbled when he noticed that Scar donned an expensive Armani suit, complete with a tailor-made French cuff shirt with diamond cuff links, and to top it off, what looked to be an authentic Cuban cigar sticking out of the breast pocket of his suit jacket.

Scar looked down at his suit and back over at Derek. Speaking with his eyes and facial expression, Scar was letting Derek know that he was still the man, regardless of the bust.

"All rise. The honorable Judge Irvin Klein presiding in the matter of the State of Maryland versus Stephon Johnson," the court officer called out. Everyone in the courtroom stood.

Derek broke his gaze on Scar, turned around, and stood as the judge slid into his seat on the bench.

With a bang of his gavel, the judge started the highly anticipated court proceedings. An eerie hush fell over the courtroom, and all eyes were front and center.

"Is the state ready to present its case? If so, prosecutor Fuller, you may begin," Judge Klein stated.

On cue, the prosecutor, who Derek thought was the most beautiful, sexy caramel specimen of a woman he had ever laid eyes on, stood up to start. *My wife is not only beautiful, she is on point. She got this shit,* Derek thought to himself, smiling proudly. She moved her sexy frame from behind the table and opened her mouth, but before she could speak, Scar's defense lawyer, a shark named Larry Tillman, jumped to his feet.

"Your Honor, I would like to move to have this case dismissed immediately," Mr. Tillman announced.

Everyone in the courtroom was looking at him like he was crazy. Not only was he interrupting the prosecutor, he was stepping on the toes of one of the most hard-ass judges in the Maryland court system. Hushed murmurs passed amongst the onlookers.

"Mr. Tillman, you will speak when spoken to," Judge Klein said.

"Your Honor, with all due respect, I am requesting to approach the bench," Mr. Tillman said.

Prosecutor Fuller looked around, confused. She was seething mad. This wasn't supposed to be happening. She ran her hands over her skirt and cocked her head to the side in an attempt to compose herself.

"Your Honor, please tell me you will not allow the defense to turn this trial into a sideshow," she said through clenched teeth.

"Approach!" the judge yelled.

Derek looked around and saw that Scar was smiling from ear to ear. The members of the media were going crazy, writing and recording.

The two attorneys approached the bench. The judge leaned in and spoke to them, while everyone else seemed to be holding their breath, waiting to see what would happen next.

Finally, the judge spoke somberly. "Mr. Tillman, you may proceed with your argument for dismissal," the judge said.

"I would be glad to," Tillman replied, smiling like a Cheshire cat.

"Your Honor, with all due respect, I am asking that the state's case against my client, Stephon Johnson, be dismissed, and that the evidence obtained be deemed inadmissible, as it was obtained with an illegal warrant. My client was arrested inside the house at the address 245 Covington Lane. The warrant used to illegally search my client's property was granted for the address 254 Covington Lane—a completely different, and might I add, nonexistent address. Therefore, it was obtained through an illegal search and seizure, which you and I both know was a direct and despicable violation of my client's rights.

"The state and their rogue cowboy troopers showed no writ of probable cause to enter my client's property and seize property or persons contained therein. This case was a prime example of the Maryland State Police's constant attempt at racial profiling and prejudice against young men like my client. I move to have this case dismissed without prejudice and expunged from my client's record," Mr. Tillman argued.

Tiphani Fuller looked back at her husband, contorting her face with anger. *He told me it would all be good. This better not come back to haunt my career,* she thought.

Loud gasps and murmurs erupted in the courtroom as Scar's attorney laid out his argument. Derek gripped the bottom of the wooden bench so hard that his knuckles turned white. He knew Scar would be released, but his lawyer was supposed to let the trial go on for a while first, to help Derek score a few more points with the chief. Making himself, his wife, and the department look bad had never been part of the plan. This was supposed to be a win-win for everyone, but Tillman was flipping the script.

Chief Scott and the entire unit sat in the back of the courtroom. They were up in arms as they heard the defense basically make them look like racist assholes. Scar just sat there with a smug look on his face, knowing he was about to be set free.

"Order! Order!" Judge Klein screamed out, banging his gavel over and over. Finally, things quieted down in the courtroom. "In light of this new and unsettling revelation and the fact that the court records reflect the address on the warrant is in fact the wrong one, I have no choice but to honor the U.S. Constitution, in accordance with the fourth amendment, which provides citizens the right to be free from illegal search and seizure. I hereby dismiss the State's case against defendant Stephon Johnson on the grounds that the State's evidence is inadmissible in the nature it was obtained," Judge Klein said regretfully, slamming his gavel and rushing up from the bench.

The courtroom erupted into pandemonium. Reporters scrambled to get the best shots of Derek and Scar. Tiphani threw her papers on the desk and stood up, enraged. The narcotics unit members and Scar's henchmen began exchanging harsh words, and the court officers were overwhelmed with trying to bring order in the courthouse.

Derek hung his head in shame. His wife shot him evil looks. This was no longer part of the act. She had put her ass on the line for this case, and she was truly pissed off now.

Chief Scott rushed over to him and grabbed him by the arm. "I need to talk to you, Detective Fuller . . . now!" he growled, pulling Derek into the hallway by his arm. "For Christ's sake, Fuller, what the fuck were you thinking? Something as simple as the right address on a fucking warrant!" Chief Scott said in a harsh whisper.

"I told Cassell two forty-five. I even wrote it down for him. I can't help it if he's dyslexic and can't write the right number!" Derek lied. The truth was he didn't write it down, and Cassell had written the address correctly. Derek just went back and reversed the numbers. He had failed to factor Scar's pain-in-the-ass lawyer into the equation, and now things had blown up in his face.

"Chief, I can fix this," Derek started.

"You let the department down. You better come up with some good shit to redeem yourself, Fuller," Chief Scott said.

Just then a huge, uproarious crowd began moving toward them. It was like the scene around a hot celebrity surrounded by fans.

Derek and the chief looked on and saw Scar in the middle of the crowd. He could not contain the still-smug smile that spread across his face as he rolled his unlit Cuban cigar between his fingers. As the crowd, complete with media cameras and Scar's henchmen, approached Derek, Scar stopped.

"If it ain't the fuckin' man without a plan," Scar said sarcastically to Derek, winking.

That was it.

"Fuck you!" Derek screamed, lunging at Scar. He instinctively reached to his waistband for his weapon, but felt nothing there. When he entered the courthouse, he'd had to check in his gun.

"You lucky bastard," Derek grumbled as Chief Scott blocked him. This take down was supposed to make Derek look good, and now Scar was standing here in front of all the cameras, rubbing shit in Derek's face. This was not the way things were supposed to go down, and if Derek didn't know better, he'd say that Scar was enjoying this a little too much.

Scar's crew had gotten ready for battle, stepping in front of Scar, ready to take on Derek. Chief Scott continued to struggle to restrain Derek.

"Fuller! This bastard is not fucking worth it," the chief said, dragging a raging Derek down the opposite end of the courthouse hallway. Scar popped his collar and stepped across the courthouse threshold into freedom.

The show looked good, and everyone was completely fooled, except one lone person, who sat in the back of the courtroom and witnessed the whole circus act. From the moment they saw Scar's lawyer argue the fourth amendment and the little wink that Scar gave Detective Fuller after the trial, the observer knew something was not right. It was now time to find out exactly what was going on.

Chapter 3

Things Are Not Always What They Seem

Scar's custom built mansion sat on almost twenty acres in an affluent Baltimore suburb. The circular driveway was filled with every luxury car on the market. There was no mistaking his wealth because he flaunted it relentlessly. Music could be heard blaring from beyond the huge wrought-iron gates. Scar wanted to celebrate every day for the same amount of time he was locked up awaiting trial. This was just day one of his planned festivities.

Inside of his twenty thousand square foot home, Scar sat on his custom-made throne in his very own champagne room. He watched as two beautiful, exotic model-type chicks performed a striptease in front of him and his newest recruits—Trail, Sticks, and Flip. Scar was in the process of grooming the three young heads to be as deadly as he was at their age. He trained his little henchmen much like dogfighters trained their pit bulls to become deadly killers, with harsh treatment and just enough food—or in the young heads' case, money—to keep them loyal to him. They were the next generation of his Dirty Money Crew.

Scar sat surrounded by bottles of Moët and Cristal and stacks of money. He was definitely back at his best. He held his customary Cuban between his pointer and middle fingers and laughed. "Yo, the black bitch got a donkey ass. I would murder that pussy," Scar said as he tossed hundred dollar bills at the women's naked bodies.

"Nigga, you ain't never lied," Trail replied, touching his crotch for emphasis.

Scar took a bottle of Moët Rose to the head. He was feeling good. As Scar drank, there was a knock at the door.

Scar slammed his drink on the table and furrowed his brow. "Yo, who the fuck is that breaking up my private party? Niggas know I don't like to be disturbed when I'm in my champagne room," Scar complained.

"A'ight, I'ma take care of that," Sticks replied, pulling his .357 Magnum from his waistband and heading toward the door.

Trail and Flip also pulled their weapons. Sticks pulled back the door to reveal the unlucky bastard who decided to encroach on their good time. Everybody aimed their weapons at the culprit guilty of breaking up Scar's private party.

"I fuckin' surrender, damn!" the man at the door said, throwing his hands in the air.

"Nigga, you must got a death wish!" Sticks said, lowering his gun when he recognized who was at the door. Everyone else followed suit, and Scar immediately lightened his mood too.

"It's all good. This here the only nigga I would let slide for fucking up my moment," Scar announced at the sight of the man. Scar smiled wide. It did his heart good to see the dude.

"Damn, nigga, you gonna have your dudes put me on ice and shit," Derek said, laughing and walking over to Scar to give him a pound and a chest bump.

"Yo, nigga. Detective fucking Fuller. I gotta tell you what, your ass deserve a fuckin' Academy Award for all that acting you did during that fuckin' bust and at the courthouse. Your ass was better than Will Smith and shit," Scar said, chuckling at his own joke. "That fucking arrest was very believable. You said all the shit those fuckin' pigs be saying: 'Shut the fuck up! Stand the fuck up!' Then at the courthouse you acted like you was really gonna kick my ass and shit. Talking all that blah, blah . . . I would hire you to be in my movies any day, nigga," Scar continued, cracking up.

"Was I good or what?" Derek asked as he got comfortable. He picked up Scar's bottle of Moët and took a swig, knowing in his head that not all of his anger was an act. Some of that shit was real, but he wasn't going to let Scar know he was pissed that the lawyer ended the trial so fast.

The Dirty Money Crew was kind of taken a-back at how easygoing Scar was around Derek.

"The whole 'son of a bitch' thing had me rolling too. I was thinking, shit, if I'm a son of a bitch, you a straight son of a bitch too, since we from the same bitch," Scar continued, laughing hard at his own jokes.

"You owe me for them days up in the clink. I'ma have to take some dough off the top," Scar said jokingly. He really looked at his time before the trial as a small sacrifice for a bigger payoff later.

"Don't play! I'm the one who should get extra pay for letting you fuck up my good name. I had to look big-time stupid and embarrassed for fuckin' up the warrant and shit. I don't even know how they fuckin' believed a debonair, sharp-ass nigga like me would fuck up a warrant. But that was some genius shit you came up with, my man, changing the numbers around. It's also a good thing I got my wifey on lock so I could convince her to go through with it," Derek said.

This wasn't the first time Derek had botched a drug bust, so he had to come up with a good plan for how to do it again. This time had to be different from last time, even though last time was a true fuck-up. He had legitimately forgotten to get a warrant a few years back while busting Scar's rival, a drug dealer named Malek. Scar had wanted his competition stomped and destroyed, and Fuller and his crew were more than willing to oblige in order to keep their share of the drug profits padding their pockets. Only problem was that in their eagerness to take Malek out, they forgot to follow the rules. So, Malek lived to sling another day, and Derek and his crew looked like chumps. That's the problem with working on that side of the law: those fucking rules get in the way.

"Yo, I'ma bounce." Derek didn't want to take a chance on anyone seeing him there. Scar wanted to meet in a few days at their normal spot, a small Italian restaurant in Bowie, a suburb of Baltimore, but Derek just couldn't wait. He knew coming to Scar's house this soon after the trial was risky, but not seeing his brother since the bust had Derek missing him big time.

"We make a good fucking team, bro. You keep the law up off me, I keep your pockets laced, you use me to look like a hero cop, I use you to buy myself a lot of time before any other five-O even thinks twice about busting up on me, for fear that my high-paid lawyer will make them look like shit. Nigga, it all worked out," Scar explained, extending his hand to offer Derek one of his prized Cuban cigars.

Derek took the little gift and nodded in agreement at what Scar was saying. He understood the being made to look like shit part, but that was the one thing that Derek had a hard time accepting. He had to admit that the money he made from helping Scar evade the law was more than he could ever dream of seeing from his state salary. But sometimes living a double life took its toll on him mentally, especially because of his special connection to Scar.

"Flip, give this man what he came for," Scar instructed, waving his hand like Flip was his servant.

"You wanna get up on that donkey ass right there before you go home?" Scar asked Derek, gesturing toward the strippers.

"Nah, I got a beauty at home. She's all I need," Derek said, thinking about his wife.

Scar smiled wide, almost smirking. He could never understand how a man could love one woman to the extent that Derek loved his wife. Scar thought Derek almost seemed like a punk for her.

"I hear that, nigga. That got to be some good-ass shit if you gon' pass up that J-Lo ass right there. By the way, tell my sister-in-law I said hello," Scar commented with that smirk appearing on his face again.

Before Derek could respond, Flip returned and reluctantly handed Derek a black duffel bag filled with cash. It was the profit from their last cocaine flip. When Scar had told his young soldiers they had to give up their last flip, they weren't too happy. Flip was the most upset. Scar had decided to give Derek the entire profit. The crew thought it was like a slap in the face, since they were the ones on the front line putting in the work. They didn't think that

Derek's help was anywhere near as important to the operation as their grinding. But none of them dared to question Scar. Not right now anyway.

Flip gave up what he thought of as his loot, but he filed it in his mental Rolodex. He had a plan.

Derek took a quick look inside the bag and looked back at Scar a bit confused. It was more than he had ever seen in his dealings with Scar. A line of sweat broke out on Derek's forehead as his mind raced with ideas on how he would "wash" all that money to make it look legit before he could spend it.

"Yeah, I thought you deserved a little extra. I mean, we are brothers, right?" Scar said seriously.

"Yeah, blood of my blood, flesh of my flesh, nigga for life," Derek said in an almost inaudible whisper. Seeing all that money gave Derek an uneasy feeling, almost as if he was getting in too deep. He wasn't about to go back on his promise to his mother now, though, so he put that uneasy feeling right out of his mind.

"That's what I'm saying, nigga. We blood for life, so when I can look out, I will. That bond is important," Scar commented.

Derek nodded. He was feeling a strong sense of love and allegiance. He never wanted to be separated from his brother again. Derek closed the bag, gave his brother a hug, and headed home to his wife.

Once he was outside of Scar's doors, Derek slid behind the steering wheel of his car, and with his heart racing, he checked the bag of money again. He rested his head on the head-rest and thought about what he had done and had been doing for the past two years. He felt so caught in the middle sometimes. Derek loved his brother, but he knew this shit was all going to come to an end one day; however, right now he didn't see a way out.

Brother or not, Derek knew Scar was dangerous. When he had been reunited with his brother, Derek was so excited to find him after their tragic childhood separation that he overlooked Scar's life of crime. It wasn't long before he had been drawn into a web of lies and deceit. He felt an overwhelming need to stay connected and bonded to Scar, the only piece of his mother and his true identity that he had left. He had made his mother a promise that he would take care of his little brother—no matter what. Derek was determined to keep that promise. He felt it would keep his mother's memory alive in his heart and mind. Derek closed his eyes, and just like always, the memories flooded back.

In a car across the street from Scar's house, the observer from the courtroom had watched Detective Fuller enter the house and come out with a duffel bag. The person immediately picked up a cell phone and started taking pictures. After the trial, or rather the theatrical event at the courthouse, the lone spectator decided to take a trip to Scar's house and see what was going on. Little did they know that Detective Fuller would be there, entering the house of his enemy so soon after the trial. Even more interesting to the person was the detective leaving with the duffel bag.

Derek pulled away from the house, and his new shadow put down the cell phone and prepared to follow. Before they could pull away from the curb, a dark blue Chevy Impala pulled up. The shadow stayed put so as not to draw any attention. Keeping as still possible, the observer watched as a tall black man with salt-and-pepper hair stepped out of the Chevy.

"That dude look familiar. Where do I know him from? Better take some pictures to document this shit for later perusal," the shadow said, picking up the phone and snapping a few pictures as the familiar-looking dude walked into Scar's house. This shit was definitely getting interesting.

Chapter 4

The Past Dictates the Future

"Mommy! Ahhhh!" Derek screamed, his small, cherubic face turning almost burgundy as he jumped up and down in sheer terror. His brother stood next to him and peed on himself as he watched too.

"I told you before, bitch, you don't play with my fuckin' money!" a strange man screamed as he dragged their mother by her hair. The man was so big and his skin was so black that he looked to Derek like a giant monster.

As the boys screamed, the man hoisted their mother in the air by her throat. Derek felt vomit creep up his throat and his bowels threatened to release from the fear he felt. His mother clawed at the man's hands in a futile attempt to loosen his grip so she could breathe.

"Get off my mommy!" Stephon screamed, the scar he was born with dragging the side of his mouth down, causing his words to slur. Derek grabbed onto his little brother's shirt and pulled him back. He couldn't risk this monster harming his brother too.

"Please don't hurt my babies," their mother rasped, begging the man for mercy.

"Bitch, you should have thought about that before you decided to cross me," the giant said, hoisting her up and throwing her up against the wall. She hit the wall with a thud and slid down, her body going limp like a rag doll. She continued to scream and beg for her life as the man pounded on her.

He let his fist land at will, each punch harder than the one before. "You like to smoke crack? You like to steal from people, bitch?" the man growled as he lifted her weak body so he could get to her face easier. With the force of a Mack truck, he backhanded her, and one of her teeth shot from her mouth. Blood covered her face and the floor around her. "Now, I expect to get my money by tomorrow, or you and these bastard trick babies of yours gonna be dead," the man said, spewing a wad of spit on her crumpled form.

Five-year-old Derek and his four-year-old brother Stephon cowered in a corner. Derek, being a year older, tried to shield his brother from harm as usual. Although he was only five, Derek often acted as if he were ten or eleven. On the nights his mother disappeared or stayed holed up in her bedroom with different men, Derek would pour cereal or make a sandwich out of whatever was there for him and his little brother. He would make sure his brother washed his face and brushed his teeth before they went to bed.

Derek always protected Stephon, who his mother had nicknamed Scar because of his misshapen head and the scar that dragged down one side of his face, making his head resemble a boulder. "Scar, Scar . . . Scar head baby," she would sing to her youngest son. She would call Derek her "baby genius" and tell him he was destined for greatness.

People often thought the brothers were fraternal twins because they were the same size. Although Scar was a year younger, he was always just as big as his older brother.

When he was sure the giant was gone, Derek got up and went to his mother's side. "Mommy?" he whined, nudging her frantically. When she didn't respond, he thought she was dead for sure. "Mommy!" he called out again, with urgency rippling through his words.

Finally, his mother shifted, winced in pain, moaned, and turned over. Struggling to get up and barely able to speak through her swollen lips, she rushed her boys to put on their coats. Afraid and visibly shaken, Derek followed his mother's instructions and helped Scar into his coat and put on his own. Their mother rushed them out of the apartment, looking around nervously the entire time.

Once they were outside, their battered mother let motherly instinct take over. She ignored the massive pains ripping through her entire body as she walked at a feverish pace to get her children far away from the potential danger.

Derek could keep up, but Scar had a hard time, and he gasped for breath because he had to jog just to keep in step. After walking for what seemed like an eternity, the trio finally came to a middle class white neighborhood.

"Go in there and y'all stand right by that green dumpster. Don't move until I come back. You hear me, Derek?" his mother said, her words garbled and her face becoming more swollen by the minute.

"When you coming back?" Derek asked, shivering anxiously.

"Take care of your brother, okay? He is special, and don't you let nobody bother him about his face. You hear me?" she said, ignoring his question as her body quaked with sobs.

"When you coming back?" Derek asked her again, an ominous feeling taking over.

"Just take care of your brother," his mother said, shoving them along.

As they started ambling forward slowly toward the dumpster, their mother turned and limped away as fast as she could. Her heart was breaking as she walked farther and farther away from her children. She knew eventually somebody would find them and take care of them. If she kept them, she feared, her addiction would eventually get them killed.

Scar began crying out, "Mommy! Mommy! Don't leave us."

"Shhh. Mommy is coming back. I'm gonna take care of you until she comes back," Derek consoled, squeezing his brother's hand tightly.

Derek took his brother and stood right where his mother had instructed him. They stood at the dumpster until the sun came up. Their legs throbbed and Scar whined and cried in between nodding from sleep deprivation. Derek refused to sit down or allow Scar to sit down. His mother had told him to stand there, and he would not let her down. Several people passed them and stared, but no one said anything to them. It was the trash truck driver who came to empty the dumpster who finally asked Derek why they were there.

"My mommy said she is coming back for us," Derek said. After waiting with Derek and Scar for three hours, the trash man finally called the authorities.

Derek never saw his mother again. When the child protective service workers and the police showed up, Derek still refused to move. They had to finally, forcefully remove him from the dumpster.

"No! I'm waiting for my mommy! No!" Derek screamed and kicked. It was to no avail. Derek and Scar were whisked away to the hospital for a medical clearance and then off to foster care.

The boys remained in foster care for more than a year, but with the mandatory expiration on parental rights, after eighteen months they were put up for adoption. Every Wednesday, Derek and Scar went to the agency along with about twenty-five other kids, to be on display for prospective parents. Derek would always hold Scar's hand and tell people that they were not being separated and if they wanted him, they would have to take Scar too. With one look at Scar's disfigured face, the potential parents always turned away and found other kids to adopt.

Derek's plan had worked for weeks, and each week, Derek and Scar would go together back to the foster home. After a few weeks of this flat out rejection, the social workers couldn't figure out why at least one of the boys could not attract an adoptive family. The workers finally started sitting close to Derek and Scar. When the workers got wind of what Derek was doing, the next Wednesday, they put Derek and Scar in separate rooms. Derek was picked immediately. He was seven, with the cutest dimples and the prettiest smile. Scar, on the other hand, had been overlooked again and again.

The day Derek's new family—a father who was a cop and a mother who was a teacher— came to pick him up, he refused to leave without his brother. He fought and cursed and even locked himself inside the bathroom. The social workers lied to Derek in order to coax him out of the bathroom so his new parents could grab him and get him home.

"Your brother will be coming along soon. Go ahead. You will see him again," she said.

Not fully believing her, but also not wanting to do anything that would possibly delay his brother's departure, Derek reluctantly went. He wouldn't see his brother until almost fifteen years later, when they had both landed on opposite sides of the law.

In Derek's new adoptive home, everything seemed to be perfect. His father fought crime and his mother taught him everything there was to know in any book imaginable. They were a real family. They ate dinner together and had fun movie nights on Fridays, his father's day off. Derek lived like a kid that had been born with a silver spoon in his mouth. He wore the finest clothes, had every toy before it even became popular with other kids, and most of all, he had a real family life—with both parents. But despite how it seemed from the outside, everything wasn't as peachy as it seemed.

Derek's father worked the midnight shift, and when he left home at ten o'clock after tucking his son in and kissing his wife, things would take a dark turn in the house. Derek's adoptive mother would creep into his bedroom at night and wake him up. She would shake him awake and stand over him wearing a see-through nightgown. Longing for her husband's touch and affection, Mrs. Fuller was lonely and desperate. She would climb into bed with her adopted son and stroke his hair. Then she would tell Derek that she loved him more than anything in the world.

She knew the one thing that was most important to Derek, and she used it against him. Mrs. Fuller told him that if he wanted to see his brother again, he would have to touch her, and she would help him find his brother.

Derek was so desperate to see Stephon again that he would have done anything his adoptive mother asked of him. At first it started out as touching; she would take his little hands and guide them around her body, making Derek touch her breasts and put his fingers in her vagina. By the time Derek was eleven, she had begun to make him have full-blown intercourse with her. She would always perform fellatio on him first, then make him perform cunnilingus on her. Then she would take his still growing penis and force him to put it in her oversized, sloppy pussy.

Most of the time, Derek felt disgusting and dirty, but he so longed for his brother that he ignored it and did what he was told. Sometimes he wanted to vomit. But things changed, and he felt differently as the years went by.

His body would betray him and he started to experience sensations that he did not quite understand. Derek tried to fight the "good feeling" that he started to get as he got older, but soon realized that the faster he got to that feeling the better, because his nightmare would then be over. Derek would ejaculate after a few minutes so he wouldn't feel so guilty. It was ingrained in him as a coping mechanism; cum quickly and it will be over, he used to tell himself. It had become a way of life for him.

Derek had everything any child could want: toys, a private school education, and church every Sunday. Even with everything, he endured torture for years. The only thing Derek wanted was to see his biological mother and brother again.

On the other hand, still in the hood of Baltimore, Scar remained in the foster care system. After years of teasing and beatings at the hands of other kids in group home after group home, Scar grew angry inside. On most days he felt ruthless, and often had visions of killing the social workers and the other kids with his bare hands. It wasn't long before Scar was on edge.

"Hey, elephant man," a boy had called out to Scar, throwing a ping pong ball from the day room, hitting Scar in the head. Scar bit down into his cheek and ignored his tormentor. "You so ugly we could probably win a world war just by showing your face to the enemies," the boy continued, garnering laughs from the other kids sitting around. "Look at that scar and those saggy lips. I bet your mother must have fucked a gorilla to get something as ugly as you," the boy said, letting out a shrill, grating laugh.

That was it. Scar's ear seemed clogged, and the room started spinning around him. He snapped. He never tolerated anyone talking about his mother or his brother. "Arrrggh!" Scar screamed out, suddenly lunging at the boy. Scar gripped a pocket knife he had stolen from the local sporting goods store.

The boy's eyes popped open in shock. He had not expected the "ugly monster kid" to ever fight back. The boy backed up from Scar's contact. He was holding his throat and gagging. Screams erupted in the room, and some of the other kids ran out into the hallway to get help. Scar had buried the pocket knife deep into the boy's neck, hitting his jugular vein.

Scar stumbled backward at the sight of his deed. Thick burgundy blood—arterial blood—spewed from the boy's neck like a fountain.

With every pump of his heart, the boy lost what looked like a half pint of blood.

Before any of the group home administrators could help, the boy had bled to death within minutes, right at Scar's feet. Although he was scared to death, something inside of Scar felt powerful, almost invincible. He had learned how to silence his tormentor. He was never going to let anyone disrespect him again.

The group home security tackled Scar to the floor and held him there until the police arrived. After the incident, Scar spent two months in a mental institution. When the psychiatrist cleared him, Scar was placed in a juvenile detention center, where he stayed until he was eighteen years old.

The detention center was where Scar learned all of his criminal ways. When he was released onto the streets of Baltimore, instead of being rehabilitated, Scar had become a ruthless dude with a nothing-to-lose attitude.

Derek went away to college, and only returned to his adoptive home when his father was laid to rest after a long battle with cancer. He felt he needed to pay his respects. He didn't hold a grudge against his adoptive father for the abuses that happened. After all, he never told his father about any of it, so how could Derek expect him to do anything about it?

When the funeral was over, Derek told his adoptive mother that she would never see him again. He had never forgiven her for years of sexual abuse. In fact, it had followed him like a looming nightmare. Derek had always felt like he had no control over his own body or his own sexuality. When he began having sex for pleasure with girls his age, his body would betray him. His mind would overpower his physical will not to ejaculate quickly.

Derek immediately moved back to Baltimore. Maybe, just maybe, he thought, he would run into his real mother or his brother. After a year of looking for corporate jobs, Derek joined the Maryland State Police.

After a while. Derek gave up the active search to find his mother and brother again. He didn't know the first place to look. Checking the foster care system had turned up nothing on Scar. The records were sealed on kids who aged out of foster care anyway. Then one day, as a highway patrol trooper, Derek walked into the squad room of the narcotics unit to get a white powder test done on a substance he had seized during a car stop, and right on the wall was a huge

WANTED poster with his brother's face and name plastered on it. It read: STEPHON "SCAR" JOHNSON, REWARD $10,000.

Derek stared at the picture for what felt like ten minutes. He was so overcome with emotion; he didn't know whether to laugh, cry, scream hallelujah, or kiss the poster. When it had finally sunken in that the man in the picture was really Scar, Derek's little Scar head brother, Derek got so nauseated and weak he almost threw up.

"What's the matter, Fuller? You look like you saw a ghost in that mu'fucka Scar Johnson," one of his colleagues asked.

"Nah, nah. Just looking around," Derek said, quickly pulling himself together before anyone caught on to his interest in Scar.

After seeing that picture, Derek was hopeful again, and he set out to find his brother. It had never occurred to him before that he could use his police resources to try to find his brother and mother.

When he pulled Scar's criminal history, he learned just what his brother had been doing since he last saw him at five years old. Scar had a rap sheet as long as a city block. Derek learned that Scar had become the founder of the notorious Dirty Money Crew, a crew of killers that had murdered their way to the top of the Maryland drug trade.

Derek was on the other side of the law, but the fact still remained that Scar was his blood, and he had been determined to find him one day. Derek worked hard to prove himself as the best trooper on the streets just so he could get enough clout in the department to put in his application to join the drug team. He was a man on a mission.

After six months, Derek made the narcotics force. He had officially become a jump out boy. Every time Derek went on a jump out operation to pick up the hand-to-hand street pharmacists, he was hopeful he would run into Scar or get some information on him. Finally, Derek and his team jumped out on a set of corner boys, and it just so happened that the little dudes they picked up were down with the Dirty Money Crew. They were low men on Scar's payroll.

It didn't take long for Derek to get one of them alone and promise him freedom if he told him where to find Scar. At first, the little soldier was living by the street creed: No Snitching! But the longer the boy sat in a cell, unable to use the bathroom, get anything to eat, and with no phone calls, he finally gave in and provided Derek with the information he needed.

Derek sat outside of all of Scar's trap houses for weeks, but Scar never showed up. Being out there undetected, Derek had figured out every drop off and pick up time. He had numbered Scar's workers, and used logic to figure out the one who must have been a higher-up, which meant he was probably closest to Scar. Derek noticed that the dude was the one that was the most consistent player at all of the trap houses, and he never stuck around long. Derek reasoned he was the lieutenant in charge of bringing the re-up and picking up the profits. Finally, Derek decided to tail him. Sure enough, one night Derek followed the dude right to his leader.

Derek's heart thumped wildly when he covertly peeked out of his windshield and saw Scar in the flesh. It was his long lost brother. Derek could recognize that scarred face and huge head anywhere. There he was, his little brother all grown up and the leader of a crime syndicate. It made Derek proud and sad all at the same time.

He sat there and wondered what their lives would have been like had their mother not abandoned them that fateful night. His best guess was that the big-ass man that had beaten his mother unmercifully had probably returned and killed her. When Derek was a teenager, he had convinced himself that she was probably better off dead than running the streets chasing crack.

Derek watched Scar that first night and didn't reveal himself, although he wanted to rush out of the car and embrace his brother with a big hug and a sincere apology. Derek didn't know how his brother would react to him, or if Scar would even remember him.

Conflicted, Derek went home to Tiphani, who was then his girlfriend, and confided in her his secret: he was a cop and his brother was a wanted criminal. Tiphani told Derek she wanted him to do whatever would make him happy.

For two days, Derek changed his car and disguise and watched his brother. Finally, he felt he had grown the balls to reveal himself to his brother.

Derek walked up to Katrina's, the bar and lounge that Scar owned and had named after their mother. It also housed Scar's office in a secret room in the back. Derek was stopped at the door and asked what his business was, since it was a bit early for patrons.

"I just wanna get a drink, man. Long fuckin' day," Derek said to the goons protecting the front door.

The front door man surveyed Derek, wondering if this square could be a cop or a fed.

Since he was dressed like a typical street dude, Derek was allowed entry. He ordered a few drinks and built up his courage. "He's your little brother, li'l Scar head," Derek whispered to himself.

With his liquid courage flowing, he walked to the back of the lounge. Derek encountered a tall, muscular dude, yet another layer of security.

"Yo, man, I need to see Scar," Derek said to the dude, trying to sound as street as he could. Derek had lost that edge a long time ago, so it was a stretch for him.

"Who the fuck are you, nigga?" the goon asked, trying to intimidate Derek with his snarl.

"Tell Scar I got information on his family," Derek said.

The goon crinkled his face in confusion. Everybody on the street knew that Scar always proclaimed he was born from the concrete. "No mother, no father, no family. Just a pure bred street nigga," was what he proclaimed.

"Nah, Scar ain't got no family," the goon told Derek.

"Everybody got family. Now, tell him I got information on his family," Derek said forcefully, not backing down.

Scar's security guard reluctantly went behind the secret door, which was obscured with police grade double-sided glass. Two minutes later, the man returned and asked Derek a question.

"Scar wants to know, if you got information on his family, where was his mother's birthmark?"

Derek swallowed hard because his mother's face came flooding back to his mind's eye. He could see her brown sugar–colored skin and straight white teeth so clearly smiling at him. Those memories were from a time when things were so good for them. In reality, the last time he'd laid eyes on his mother, she was a gaunt skeleton with missing teeth and riddled with bruises.

Shaking his head, Derek got it together. "It . . . it was a heart-shaped, cherry-colored mark on her left cheek, and she used to call it 'a mother's love' and tell us she got it from our kisses," Derek said, barely able to get the words out.

The man was really confused when Derek said "our kisses." He looked at Derek intensely then disappeared, armed with the answer. Within minutes, the man returned and Derek was allowed to follow him back to the secret office.

When Derek stepped into the room, it was like time stood still. Scar was sitting behind a huge mahogany desk like the CEO of a legitimate company. Scar's face looked much improved. His scar actually made him look dangerous, instead of ugly and deformed like it did when he was a kid. Who would've thought an ugly birth defect could benefit him? It was as if his deformity had dictated what he was to become.

Derek was at a loss for words. He stared at Scar, thinking his eyes were deceiving him. Derek's legs were weak and threatened to fail him.

"Ain't this a bitch! My little big brother," Scar said, standing up and stepping from behind the desk.

Derek was still speechless. Like the first time he saw the wanted poster, Derek didn't know what to do—cry, scream, or say he was sorry.

"I know the cat ain't got your tongue, nigga. You ain't happy to see your little brother after a hundred years and shit?" Scar said, grabbing Derek for a manly hug.

"I'm just so fuckin' happy to see you, man," Derek finally managed to say. "I'm so sorry I couldn't keep my promise. I was a kid. They snatched me away from you. I had promised Mommy . . ." Derek rambled, shaking all over.

"C'mon, man. I don't hold you responsible for nothin'. Them white people ain't care nothing about two black little niggas try'na keep whatever piece of family they had together. I ain't never blame you, my nig. Besides, if shit didn't happen the way it did, I wouldn't be the king that I am today," Scar assured, offering his dumbfounded brother a seat.

"I told Mommy I would always take care of you. I'm back, and I will keep that promise," Derek assured his brother. And he didn't lie. Although he had pledged allegiance to uphold the law of the state of Maryland, his allegiance to his family was stronger. Derek had another chance to keep his promise to his mother, and he vowed he would forever be his brother's keeper—that is, if his brother wanted to be kept.

From that day forward, Derek helped Scar stay above the law. He made sure Scar was always one step ahead of the jump out boys and the Narcotics Unit. But when the heat got turned up on Derek to make some big busts, he spoke with Scar and they agreed to put on their little show. Scar agreed to take a fall to help his brother look good in the eyes of the department and the public. It had all worked out—or so they hoped.

Chapter 5

A Tangled Web We Weave

Derek had daydreamed about his childhood and his reunion with Scar all the way home. He looked at the bag of dirty money he held and asked himself if it was worth it. It gave him an ill feeling in the pit of his stomach. That was a lot of fucking money, and the old street credo—more money, more problems—was about to ring true for Derek Fuller.

Shaking his head to clear out the cobwebs of the past, Derek pulled into his driveway. Thoughts of his wife and her warm hugs, kisses, and hot sex motivated him to snap the fuck out of it.

Derek crept into his house. He knew Tiphani would be in the bed, and he wanted to make everything up to her—the court thing, his recent shortcomings in the bedroom, and some of the lies he told her about where he got some of his extra money from.

Derek slowly pushed open the French doors to their bedroom. Tiphani was already asleep. He went into their walk-in closet and put his loot in the wall safe. He took off his weapon and all of his clothes.

Derek planned to wake his wife with a stiff dick and a good pussy pounding. At least he hoped that he could keep it together long enough. He got himself mentally ready. This time, he wasn't going to let himself cum too fast. He told himself he would fight the urge to ejaculate as long as he could stand it—at least until she came first. Derek stroked himself to get ready. He let a glob of spit fall into his hand, and rubbed it up and down on his dick.

"Mmm," he moaned as his manhood came to life in his hand. When he was satisfied that he was hard enough to rock his wife's world, Derek went over to the bed.

Sliding onto the bed behind Tiphani, Derek noticed that all his sexy-ass wife was wearing was a short lace camisole, no panties. Derek smiled. *She knew I was coming home to freak her.* Derek slid one of his knees between his wife's legs from behind to make room for him to get to her goods.

"Mmmm," she moaned, acting like he was disturbing her sleep.

Derek wanted to laugh. He knew she was only playing hard to get. He never knew why women did that, acting like they were asleep when they knew damn well they wanted to jump up and ride the dick.

When Derek wedged his way between her legs and had them wide enough, he slid up behind her, licked his fingers, and searched blindly under the covers for her opening. When Derek touched her, she was already wet.

"You been waiting for me, huh?" Derek whispered, even more excited now.

At that, Tiphani knew the gig was up, and she turned over, smiling. Derek climbed on top of her and took a mouthful of her left breast into his mouth. Sucking roughly at first, than softening up, Derek pleasured her. She grew even more excited, letting small gasps escape her lips.

Derek was ready, mentally and physically. He reached down and grabbed his dick. It was time. He was determined to fuck his wife like she needed to be fucked.

Derek rammed his dick into her. "Urghh," he grunted when he felt Tiphani's warm, wet flesh around his meat.

"Ohhh," she cooed, wrapping her legs around his waist and pushing back at him.

Derek lifted his ass and came back down into the soft wetness. He grunted with labored breaths. He was excited now. The smell of sex, the sounds his wife made, the tingling he felt in his loins; it all came rushing back to his mind again. These were the same things he had experienced when he was too young to understand it.

Derek tried to hurriedly push the images of his adoptive mother's face out of his mind. But the images of her face, contorted with prohibited pleasure, kept flashing in his head.

"Yes, fuck me," Tiphani whispered.

That was enough. They were the exact words that wretched woman had said to him when he was eleven and twelve and thirteen. "Ahhhhh!" Derek screamed out as he fought a losing battle with his mind. His body involuntarily bucked and jerked against Tiphani's, and she was left disappointed.

She knew right away that Derek had ejaculated prematurely again. Tiphani looked at the clock when they'd started, and it had read 11:43. She looked at it now, and it read 11:53.

Ten fuckin' minutes, and subtract about eight for the tittie sucking and pussy touching, Tiphani thought. She rolled her eyes.

Derek lay on top of her, trying to get his dick hard again. "I'm so sorry, baby," he apologized as usual.

"Just get my toys. I need to cum," Tiphani said flatly, annoyed.

Derek felt like shit, but he jumped up and got his wife's vibrating dildo from her treasure box. He turned on the little device, wishing he could make her cum like the little plastic toy did.

Tiphani climaxed from her toy. It wasn't the same as the orgasms she had from a real flesh and blood dick, but she had to settle.

Tiphani turned over and gave Derek her back. She lay awake for the next two hours. She didn't know how much longer she could take it. It was fine when they first got together; it was easier to handle, and Tiphani was more willing to overlook certain "short-cummings," so to speak. She thought it would get better, but this shit was getting ridiculous. So, she lay there holding out hope that someday soon there would be a light at the end of the whack-dick tunnel.

The next morning, Derek was up extra early. Still feeling guilty, he busied himself with making Tiphani and the kids a huge breakfast of grits, bacon, sausage, eggs, and biscuits.

Tiphani had not said many words to him since the night before. After the whole embarrassing court episode, she planned to take a few days off, and didn't feel like getting out of bed. She felt that no amount of money was worth the embarrassment she had received at the hands of Scar's lawyer.

Trying to make it up to her, Derek brought Tiphani's breakfast to her. "I'm going to take the kids to school for you. You can stay in bed all day if you want," Derek said, trying anything to get her to smile so he would know she wasn't still mad.

"Thanks," she said dryly.

"I love you, Tiphani. It's going to get better," Derek said, not even sure himself. He kissed her on the forehead then turned and left.

She lay back down and pulled the comforter over her head. He had never told her about his molestation as a child. His pride wouldn't allow it. The same with his thoughts on Viagra: *Don't need no pill to make my dick hard,* he thought. Because of his silence on the subject, Tiphani did not understand the mental effects that sex had on him.

Tiphani didn't know how long she would be able to take this bullshit. She was at a real crossroads in her marriage. If she had known the true reason behind her husband's sexual failure, she would have been much more supportive, but she didn't. All she knew was that her clit throbbed all day, every day, and she needed good dick in her life.

"C'mon, you two. It's time for school," Derek said, rallying his kids and ushering them out the door.

Derek pulled out of his driveway, oblivious to the eyes that followed his every move.

As soon as she heard the car pull out of the driveway, Tiphani threw the comforter back and jumped out of the bed. She was free from that limp-dicked excuse of a husband, and now able to take care of her needs. She walked into her bathroom and turned on the shower.

Stepping inside, she let the water cascade down her sculpted, muscular body. Tiphani placed her hands on the beautifully tiled shower walls as she took the massaging showerhead down from the holder and placed the pulsing head up against her clit. Throwing her head back, she rotated the showerhead up and down against her swollen clit until she came.

It's a damn shame the showerhead can make me cum, but my husband can't, she thought to herself.

When she was done, she lathered her body, cleaned up, and turned off the water. Suddenly, she heard a noise coming from downstairs. Stopping in her tracks, Tiphani listened intently. She didn't hear anything else.

"Maybe I'm losing it," she whispered, turning back toward the sink. She reached down to turn on the faucet and *Clang!* The bathroom door flew open.

Tiphani screamed. She had no place to run. She was trapped in the bathroom. Her eyes popped open in sheer terror, and a second scream got caught in her throat as someone grabbed her forcefully from behind, placing a huge hand over her mouth.

"Mmmmm!" she tried to scream as she struggled to see her attacker. The apparent assailant ripped her towel off of her and pushed her up against the sink in a doggie style position.

She moaned, barely able to breathe. The next thing she felt was a sharp pain stabbing through her vagina as the stranger forcefully penetrated her from behind. He drove his dick into her with brute force, and then removed his hand from her mouth.

"Oh, shit!" Tiphani moaned in sudden ecstasy.

"You like when I fuck you rough?" he growled, banging up against her over and over again.

"Oh, Scar, you fuck me so good," Tiphani huffed out as she gripped the sides of the sink. She didn't have to look at his face; she immediately recognized the feeling of his dick.

Scar pumped her from behind like he wanted to send her through the vanity mirror that hung over the sink. Tiphani loved every minute of it. She inched up onto her tiptoes so Scar could get a better angle into her soaking wet pussy.

Scar was able to sex her without coming in two minutes, and that's all that mattered to Tiphani. She was a fucking woman with needs, she reasoned, justifying her betrayal each time.

Their affair had happened so suddenly. Once she had gotten a taste of Scar's dick, she was hooked. Tiphani had to admit that Derek was the more attractive brother, but what Scar lacked in looks, he damned sure made up for in bedroom skills and dick size.

Scar pulled his dick out of her sloppy hot box and turned her around. He buried his head in her chest and licked and sucked her nipples like a baby trying to get milk.

"Oh yeah," she groaned.

Scar lifted his head to look into her beautiful face. He felt powerful. Lifting her small frame, he cupped her ass and placed her legs around him. He positioned her onto his dick and pulled her ass into him so he could bury his dick deep into her sloppy wet pussy while he carried her. Bouncing her up and down on his thick pole, Scar fucked Tiphani all the way to the bed she shared with Derek.

Tiphani was so hot and horny she forced her tongue into Scar's deformed lips and licked his tongue. She closed her eyes tight and relished the feeling of all ten inches of his swollen manhood filling the void her husband never could.

Placing her on the bed, Scar put his knees on the bed for leverage and proceeded to drive his pole in and out of her dripping wet hot box with forceful, even pumps. Her pussy made loud slurping noises. "Ah, ah, ah, ah," Tiphani called out, loud enough to wake up the neighborhood. That dick hurt so good, and she was in her glory.

"You . . . like . . . fuckin' . . . ya . . . brother . . . in . . . law?" Scar pumped into her with each word, his muscular legs and ass flexing as he used all of his strength to dig her back out.

***

Derek had gotten all the way to the kids' school before he realized he had rushed out and left his service weapon at home in his safe. That wasn't like him at all. He had been so preoccupied trying to make things up to Tiphani. "How the fuck did I leave Bessy at home?" he asked himself out loud as he made a U-turn and headed back home.

Derek didn't bother to pull into the driveway; he just pulled in front of the house and figured he'd run right inside. Twisting the lock and entering the house, Derek heard his wife's voice in a high-pitched tone, like she was in distress.

What the fuck? He furrowed his brows and listened. The sound was coming from the direction of their bedroom. Derek started rushing toward the stairs, but quickly realized it wasn't a distress call his wife was making. He had definitely heard those sounds before when he was with her.

He stopped in his tracks and listened for a long minute that seemed like an eternity. Flexing his jaw with each moan and grunt, Derek balled his fists so tight his fingernails dug half-moon-shaped craters into his palms. His heart was pounding wildly, but he seemed to be rooted to that spot. He was in shock, and his heart thundered so hard it felt as if it would rupture.

Derek did not move until he heard his wife say the words "Scar, fuck me! Fuck me, Scar!" Spurred into action by her words, Derek bolted up the remainder of the stairs as if someone had strapped a rocket to his ass. He kicked open his bedroom doors so hard one of the doors flew off the hinges.

"Oh, shit!" Scar yelled out, jumping out of Tiphani's pussy with one hop.

Tiphani fell off the bed and scrambled around on the floor, searching in vain to find something to cover herself. "Derek, wait!" she screamed, but it was too late.

Derek bulldozed into Scar with full force. Scar was caught off guard and naked, so he couldn't really defend himself properly. "Arrrggggghhh!" Derek growled out, swinging wild punches into his brother's face and body. Scar tried to gain some leverage, but Derek was a man possessed.

"You dirty mu'fucka! You traitor!" Derek screamed, landing more punches to Scar's face.

Finally, Scar had his bearings. He bucked Derek off of him and put Derek in a headlock. Scar landed some punches to the top of Derek's head.

Struggling to free himself, Derek thought back to his police academy training techniques. With his heavy work boots, he stepped on Scar's bare feet with all his might.

"Ahhh!" Scar shrieked, loosening his grip on his brother's neck.

"I'm gonna fuckin' kill both of you stinkin' mu'fuckas!" Derek bellowed, his voice a thunderbolt of anger.

"Derek, please! Let me explain!" Tiphani cried, trying to calm her husband.

"Explain! Bitch, what is there to explain?" he screamed. In all of his fury, Derek swung around and slapped Tiphani so hard she flew almost clear across the room. Blood squirted from her nose and busted lip.

"No!" she screamed, holding her face. She knew she was fighting a losing battle trying to convince her husband to calm down. She balled up into a fetal position, afraid that if she moved or said anything, her husband might beat her to death.

Derek rushed toward his closet to retrieve his weapon.

"I will kill you, mu'fucka! I'm gonna kill you!" Derek screamed out, talking to his brother and meaning every word he said.

Scar had gathered his shit and was heading down the stairs. He wasn't one to run from anyone, but he had literally been caught slipping, butt-ass naked with his gun in the car. He had been in such a rush to bang up in Derek's wife that he left his fucking gat in the car. Scar was kicking himself for being so stupid. He knew he had to get the fuck out of dodge before his brother's temper got out of control.

Derek couldn't get his weapon out of his lock box fast enough. By the time he picked up his Glock, Scar was out the door and gone.

"You fuckin' bitch! You want to fuck a criminal? My brother? Well, I hope the mu'fucka takes care of you after I'm finished destroying him!" Derek barked, standing over his wife with his gun drawn. He was so angry he knew he could shoot her right there.

Derek blinked his eyes rapidly, trying to wipe the images of killing Tiphani out of his mind. He cocked his gun and pointed it directly at her head. He wanted to shoot her; he wanted to end her life and his pain and hurt.

Finally deciding that she wasn't worth it, Derek told himself he would get them both back in a different way. He would make them suffer slowly, while he took their lives apart piece by piece. Stopping himself before he did something stupid, he moved away from Tiphani and rushed out of his home in a fury.

"Fuck being my brother's keeper. This is gonna be some Cain and Abel shit. Scar, you done fucked up now," Derek gritted out loud, like his words would somehow telepathically reach his traitorous brother's ears.

Derek stormed into the station house, pushing past all of his colleagues. Everyone was still talking about the whole warrant dustup with Scar going free, but Derek didn't even care that they were whispering about him.

"Rodriguez, Bolden, Archie, Cassell, integ room now!" Derek screamed.

All of the members of his unit looked up. They were shocked at his outburst, and they looked around like they thought he was crazy. They knew he would be mad about what happened in the courtroom, but they had never seen him this worked up before.

Apprehensively, they all filed into the small interrogation room. It was soundproof, and no one else in the station house would be able to hear what Derek had to say. He looked like a man undone. His hands were shaking, and he paced up and down the small room like he was unable to sit or stand still. He was sweating from head to toe. His dress shirt was soaked under the arms.

The entire unit looked quizzically at the scratches and red welts on his face. "Fuller, you okay?" Rodriguez asked, her face crumpled with confusion.

"Yeah, but I thought shit through, and I can't just let that fuckin' Johnson get away like that." Derek huffed out his words, barely able to catch his breath.

"I was thinking the same shit. I still don't understand how that shit went down like it did," Bolden commented, twisting his lips to the side like he was a little suspicious. In fact, all of the members of the unit were suspicious. They had all been known to take some cash from the criminals from time to time. There were plenty of times that the unit would get together in that same room and split their profit. This wasn't the first time a criminal had gone free on their watch, but it was the first time a criminal went free and they didn't see any payoff come their way.

"I want all the stops pulled out to bring this ugly mu'fucka down!" Derek screamed, slamming his flat palms on the table until they burned. He couldn't control himself; his anger was apparent.

"But what happened all of a sudden? Why the urgency today?" Cassell asked, still confused by his leader's behavior and a little pissed that he got blamed for the mix-up on the warrant. He could have sworn he wrote the address that Fuller told him.

"Were you in court yesterday? Don't ask stupid fucking questions. Just do as I say and fucking trust me for once! I want all his files pulled. I want the cold cases of the two government officials Scar Johnson allegedly put the hit on pulled and reviewed. I want y'all to scour the streets to find informants, snitches, bitches . . . whatever. I want this mu'fucka down on an airtight case.

"Two of you need to go visit that fucking lawyer too. Rough his ass up and give his ass something to mull over before he thinks about representing a walking dead man again," Derek spat. His eyes were bulged out, and the vein in his neck thumped so wildly his subordinates could see it with their naked eyes. He was talking some crazy shit to them. He wanted them to rough up a fucking defense attorney? They were all uncomfortable now. Something wasn't right and they knew it.

"We have twenty-four hours, and I want that bastard behind bars on a charge that will take care of him for life. Either that or he needs to die," Derek said with conviction before turning around and storming out of the room.

The rest of his unit looked at each other, still taken aback.

They began filing out of the room, afraid to say anything. Apparently the unit was to set out on a new mission to bring down Scar Johnson . . . like it or not.

Chapter 6

Revenge Is a Dish Best Served Cold

Scar paced back and forth in his office. He couldn't think straight. The scenario with Derek had his mind going a mile a minute. Scar's conscience was weighing heavily on him. How could he be so foul, so fucked up toward his own flesh and blood over a bitch? Scar wished he could take it back. He was immediately sorry when his brother rushed in on him and Tiphani, but it was too late then. He knew no apology could erase the image of him screwing Tiphani from his brother's mind.

Scar had never even experienced remorse in his life. He had murdered people, assaulted women, had niggas tortured, and never lost a wink of sleep. But he actually, for the first time, felt real fucked up inside about how he had hurt his brother. Not only was Derek his brother, but Derek had come back for him, had searched for him for all those years, something that Scar couldn't say he had done. Derek also kept the law off of him for all these years. Now he wasn't so sure his brother was going to play that game. Scar needed to fix this situation fast. If not, he wouldn't just lose a brother, he could lose his whole empire.

The first time he had slept with Tiphani, it was supposed to be a one-time thing. Derek had been so excited to introduce them; his baby brother and the love of his life is how Derek had characterized them. Scar had told Derek he didn't want to meet his wife because he knew she was a prosecutor and he didn't want any parts of her. Derek convinced Scar that she would be cool, and insisted they meet. He wouldn't take no for an answer. Derek wanted his baby brother to know the love of his life, especially since they had been reunited and promised never to be separated again. That promise was all a memory now. A woman had shattered the brothers' vow.

As Scar thought back, he decided it was all Tiphani's fault. That bitch! She had come on to him after only meeting him twice. She had cried to him about Derek's sexual problems. At first, Scar thought it was amusing, his big brother not being able to hold it down in the bedroom; but then he realized Tiphani wanted him to take care of her in a way Derek couldn't. She was like a fiend . . . some kind of nympho. Scar fell into her trap, and he had to admit that her beautiful face and body had not been easy to turn away. On top of that, her pussy shot was intoxicating. The best he'd ever had.

"Everybody get the fuck outta my office!" Scar barked, sending his little flunkies scrambling to get out of his way. They all fled his office in a hurry without looking back. They had noticed that his mood had been very dark for the past two days, and usually that meant somebody's head would roll.

Scar didn't really want to be alone, but he couldn't risk his workers catching on to his pity party. He also didn't want them to hear him leave yet another message on Derek's voice mail, begging for a call back. His mind was swarming with thoughts, especially thoughts of how he was going to fix shit between him and his brother before shit got out of hand.

Scar picked up his cell and dialed his brother's number again. "Yo, D, man, I'm fuckin' sick over this shit, man. I was dead-ass wrong, man. Blood is thicker than water, man. You can't pick her over me. We need to talk. There is too much shit at stake . . . for both of us. Call me, man," Scar said in a gruff voice, trying not to sound too much like he was begging, but also letting his brother know he was sorry for what he'd done.

Scar disconnected the call and continued pacing the floor. Finally his phone rang. His heart jumped. He looked at the screen and slouched his shoulders in disappointment—it wasn't his brother. Scar didn't recognize the number.

"Yo," he said into the receiver, trying to mask his disappointment.

"Watch ya back, nigga. There's a bounty on ya ugly-ass head," a deep voice said into the receiver.

He didn't recognize the voice. "Fuck you, pussy! Bring it!" Scar barked in response. It was his first instinct to lash out and show he wasn't scared. He knew it had to be Derek or someone connected to him. Scar figured no other nigga in the Baltimore area would have the fucking balls to call his phone and threaten him.

Although he didn't want to, Scar had already begun to mentally prepare himself for his brother's wrath. Now he knew he would physically have to prepare as well. Scar didn't want it to come down to war with his own blood, but he had also learned from years of hustling that there were three things in the street that niggas spilled blood over: money, bitches, and reputations.

The anonymous caller hung up the phone, pleased with the outcome. Scar acted exactly as expected, trying to act tough, but the caller could hear a little worry and confusion in Scar's voice.

The events the caller had witnessed in the few days of trailing Scar were quite interesting. First there were all of the people going in to Scar's mansion and coming out with duffel bags, and then the scene at Detective Fuller's house. The caller didn't know whose house Scar was entering that day, but it all became clear when he saw Detective Fuller enter the house and then, a few minutes later, Scar come running out in his underwear. *Holy shit!* The observer had thought. *Scar is fucking Detective Fuller's wife!*

Continuing to shadow Scar, the caller came up with the plan. After seeing the scandal at the courthouse and Fuller coming out of Scar's place with the duffel bag, it was obvious that Scar and Fuller were somehow connected. It was just a matter of finding out how. After witnessing their fight at Fuller's house, it was obvious both were vulnerable and probably not on the best of terms. It was the perfect time to stir up some shit. Somehow, the caller needed to get this war started sooner rather than later. There couldn't be a better and easier way to turn these two against each other than to have one fucking the other's wife.

I couldn't have scripted this shit any better, the caller thought just before implementing phase one of the plan.

"Pa-lease, Derek, think about this," Tiphani begged through a face full of tears. Her face was still bruised and swollen from the backhand she took from Derek. She was grabbing Derek's arms, trying in vain to block his exit from their walk-in closet. "I will get help. I promise. I'm sorry," she pleaded.

"Tiphani, move the fuck out of my way before shit gets ugly. I feel like breaking your fucking jaw right now. I'm getting my shit and I'm out of here," Derek said, yanking his arm from her grasp. "Expect to hear from my lawyer about divorce and custody, you fuckin' whore," Derek spat evilly, his words hitting her like a whip.

She doubled over with sobs wracking her body. Tiphani felt like the rug had been pulled out from under her perfect little life. She had a handsome husband, two beautiful kids, and a little something on the side to keep her satisfied. She had her cake and was eating it too. To Tiphani, it couldn't have been any more perfect.

Derek looked down at her in disgust as he stormed out of the closet and out of their bedroom. He had vowed never to return. This shit was killing him inside. Tiphani was the first woman he had ever allowed himself to really love and trust. Yes, he could admit that he had his problems sexually, but they had taken vows for better or for worse. For her to fuck his brother was the equivalent of stabbing him in the heart and twisting the knife. In Derek's eyes, there was nothing worse she could have done.

Derek dragged his bags and stopped at his kids' rooms. He kissed his sleeping children. He would let the judge set visitation for them. Derek fought back tears and exited his home for the last time.

The pain and humiliation were so great that Derek was planning to transfer to another division after he brought Scar to his knees. He needed to get as far away as possible from the mess that his life was turning into.

Throwing his stuff into the backseat, he climbed into his car. Once inside, he slammed his fist on the steering wheel repeatedly. "Scar, you are as good as fuckin' done. I will destroy you just like you have destroyed me," Derek said through clenched teeth.

Finally, the tears dropped. Realizing he had broken down, Derek wiped his face roughly, clearing the tears before anyone could see him crying like a bitch.

He picked up his phone and called Rodriguez. He and Rodriguez had the closest relationship out of any of the members of Derek's unit. Derek figured he'd lay low with Rodriguez until he was done reigning terror on Scar.

With a new fervor for revenge, Derek screeched away from the curb outside of his former home.

That night, Derek sat at a local watering hole with his unit. He downed at least seven tumblers of Hennessy and a bunch of shots of Patrón—so many that they'd all stopped counting. Derek had intended to drink his hurt away, but as always, the alcohol seemed to make shit worse. Derek was blitzed, and he started shouting out all of his business to anyone who would listen.

"I gave that bitch my life. She fucked around on me," he slurred. "Do you know she wanted me to fuck her six times a day? She was probably fuckin' one of you guys. I wouldn't put it past her," he continued, sounding like a drunken sailor. "Who was it? You, Cassell? Huh? Did you fuck my wife? Or . . . or maybe it was Archie! Yeah, fuckin' pretty Puerto Rican bastard, it was you!" Derek stammered, pointing a wavering finger at his subordinates.

"C'mon, Fuller. I know you're hurt, but don't tell your business in here," Rodriguez told him, realizing her boss was fucked up and talking out his ass.

Derek became incensed and continued shouting. "Don't tell me what to do! You mu'fuckas need to get to work! I want that fucking Scar Johnson killed! Fuck him! Fuck sending him to jail; I got a bullet with his fucking name on it!" Derek belted out, slurring all of his words.

"Shhhh. Fuller, are you fuckin' crazy? You don't know who's in here that got connections to that dude," Cassell said, looking at his other unit members for an explanation. "This fucking dude is out of control. We better get him out of here before he gets us all killed," Cassell commented, sliding off of his barstool and pulling out his phone to make a call.

They couldn't figure out what the hell Derek's wife fucking around on him had to do with his case against Scar Johnson. They were already working hard to put shit into place to try once again to bring Scar down, but Derek's outburst just seemed random and sudden. They all exchanged confused and telling glances, finally deciding that their leader was just distraught over his wife's infidelity and that work was getting to him. They figured once he slept off his drinks he would be fine.

"C'mon, Derek. You've had enough for one night," Rodriguez said. She threw Derek's arm around her shoulder as Cassell, Archie, and Bolden helped Rodriguez steady Derek and get him into her car.

"I want immediate reports on the Johnson case tomorrow." Derek garbled his words and hiccupped at the same time.

"Yeah, Fuller. We'll brief you when you can understand English," Cassell joked.

"That's good. That's good," Derek said, his words even more garbled and jumbled than before. Derek stretched out in the back of Rodriguez's car and slept all the way to her house.

His outburst in the bar had definitely been overheard and immediately relayed back to the interested parties. The streets were always talking, and this incident was no different. Derek was oblivious that his battle cries had definitely been heard.

Scar flexed his jaw when he received more than one hood news report that a cop had been in a public bar screaming out instructions to destroy and even kill him. The one report that pissed him off the most was the phone call from the same nigga that called anonymously to warn him to watch his back. This mu'fucka was starting to get on Scar's nerves. That was the first report he received, and it seemed to Scar like it was given to him right after the cop had said it. Scar immediately knew the cop was Derek. Scar was tired of trying to cop a plea to his brother and play nice. There were but so many white flags Scar was willing to raise. A truce was obviously not what his brother was looking for.

"If this mu'fucka was fuckin' his own wife right, I wouldn't have to. I bet he don't know his bitch is begging me to come over to the house he pays mortgage for and fuck her right now. At first I felt bad, but you know what? The pussy ain't half bad. I'm taking the gloves off on his ass," Scar announced to his little trio of killers—Trail, Flip, and Sticks—the Dirty Money Crew.

They all snickered, thinking about Scar fucking his own brother's wife. They knew he was a foul, ruthless-ass nigga, but damn.

"I still don't know why you gave that lame all that money that time," Flip said, trying to act like he was joking, but finally letting his real feelings come to the surface about Scar giving Derek their entire cocaine flip.

Scar turned on Flip like Dr. Jekyll and Mr. Hyde. "What the fuck did you say?" Scar asked, his eyes going low and filling with malice.

"I'm just saying . . . it was . . . it was our dough," Flip stuttered, realizing he had gotten too loose with his lips. The look on Scar's face made Flip's heart speed up like galloping horses at the Kentucky Derby. He knew he had fucked up.

"Is this nigga questioning my authority?" Scar asked the rest of the crew rhetorically. Scar had a crazy look in his eyes. He had been looking that way for days now.

Sticks and Trail both shook their heads, not saying a word. They didn't want any part of what was to come.

"Yo, Scar, man . . . I was just commenting about that lame," Flip said, pleading with his eyes and trying to clean up the shit he had obviously stepped knee deep into. He tried to make light of the situation by putting a half smile on his face. That just made Scar even angrier.

"Fuck you smiling about, nigga? You think this shit here a joke?" Scar asked, moving in on the boy like an eagle getting ready to pick up a mouse.

"Give me your pistol, li'l nigga," Scar instructed calmly.

"C'mon, man . . ." Flip began, his teeth chattering.

"I said give me your fucking gun, nigga! Fuck is going on around this bitch? Now I gotta say shit twice," Scar boomed, rushing into Flip's personal space.

Flip leaned back to get his face away from Scar's hideous grill. Flip dug in his waistband and reluctantly handed Scar his gun. Scar cocked the 9 mm Glock and put it up to the young boy's head.

"Yo, Scar, man . . . I'm sorry. I will never question your authority again, man," Flip begged, tears welling up at the base of his eyes.

"You are a real bitch. You like to complain like a fuckin' woman? I'ma treat you like a bitch, too," Scar said, feeling more evil by the minute. This was just what Scar wanted. He had been looking for a way to release some of the pent-up stress he had been harboring over the situation with his brother.

Trail and Sticks were like statues, stiff and rigid. They were scared to even blink. Scar was unpredictable and they knew it. There was no way they were going to risk doing anything that would catch them the same wrath that was being brought down on Flip.

"Strip, mu'fucka!" Scar screamed. Flip furrowed his brows in confusion and didn't move. "You speak English, bitch? I said take off all of your clothes! Now! I fuckin' bought everything you got on! I am the one who provides for you like a mama and a daddy, and you wanna complain about a few dollars? Take off everything right fuckin' now!" Scar screamed, holding the gun on Flip menacingly.

Flip slowly obeyed Scar's wish. He removed his fitted cap, his Coogi leather jacket, his jeans, and his Timbs. When he was finished, he sheepishly stood in his wife beater and boxers.

"Nah, nigga, I bought ya drawers and all that shit! I want you naked as a newborn baby," Scar demanded.

Flip flexed his jaw and swallowed hard. He had to make a decision. Would he test Scar? Was Scar testing him to see how much of a man Flip was? In the end, he figured he didn't want to take a chance. He did as he was told to save his own life. He got butt-ass naked.

Scar let out a shrill laugh at the sight of Flip's skinny body. "Look, everybody! This chicken-chest nigga thought he had the balls to question me—the king! But that's all he got is balls . . . little-ass meatballs. His dick look like a Vienna sausage!" Scar yelled out, laughing at the same time. Humiliating Flip was making Scar feel more powerful by the minute.

Sticks and Trail were so terrified they wouldn't dare turn their eyes away, since Scar had told them to look. Flip just stood there humiliated, trying to use his hands to cover himself.

"Take this nigga up outta here," Scar said calmly, waving his hand and dismissing Flip like a discarded piece of trash. He never had any intention of killing the boy; he just wanted to show him who was boss.

Sticks and Trail walked over to Flip, but they didn't really want to touch him. Flip's eyes were popped open in confusion. He was still not sure if Scar was done with his game, or if he could relax. The only thing Flip knew was that he wasn't about to leave naked, so he bent down to pick up his boxers.

Bang! A shot rang out and everyone jumped. Flip let out an ear-shattering scream. He fell to the floor, holding his mangled hand, while Scar started laughing again like a maniac. The young boys were shaking all over.

"I said you had to leave, but not with the shit I bought," Scar explained.

Flip pulled himself up, holding his wound. His face was contorted with pain. Now Flip was unable to control the tears as the pain ripped through the bones in his fingers. Scar had shot him in the hand when he tried to touch the clothes. He was gritting his teeth and squeezing his hand, trying to stop the bleeding. Flip wanted to curse the shit out of Scar, but he knew that if he said one thing to Scar, it would probably be his last. His shit was aching so bad Flip was sure he'd lose all of his fingers.

Sticks and Trail, not wanting to be the next victims, hurriedly escorted a naked and injured Flip out onto the street. Flip had no way to get home, no money, no car keys. All of the cars the three of them drove were on loan from Scar. He basically owned them and controlled their every move. He gave them just enough material things to keep them dependent on him. Basically, Flip was fucked. He walked slowly out the door, the pain causing his body to go into shock.

People on the street stared at a bleeding and naked Flip. In his mind, Flip vowed revenge. "This mu'fucka thinks he's God . . . you fuckin' wait," he cried and mumbled as he walked along, naked as a jaybird, trying to figure out how the fuck he would get home.

Derek had made his third appearance in family court against his wife. The first two times were just to establish what they would be fighting each other for, and for each of them to hire the highest profile lawyers they could find. Today was different. Derek definitely had a strategy.

This time, the gloves had definitely come off in family court in front of the presiding judge and both of their lawyers. Derek had spilled his wife's business about her affair and her constant need for sex to the judge and any other people who had decided to come to their custody hearing. This was definitely making Tiphani livid, since a lot of people in the court-room were her colleagues. She tried hard to hold onto her composure and some sliver of her dignity while her husband aired her dirty laundry.

Derek had described her constant need for sex, and how he had walked in on her having sex right in their own home where they were raising their children. Tiphani had kept her head held high while her husband degraded her in public, but it wasn't easy. She wanted to run away and bury her head in the sand.

The only detail Derek left out was that the person Tiphani was caught with was Scar Johnson. He knew that it wouldn't be good for either of them to be associated with the most notorious gangster in Maryland. But if he could have somehow mentioned it without getting himself connected, you know damn well Derek would have sold that bitch out in a heartbeat.

At the end of the hearing, the judge entered a temporary order giving Derek and Tiphani shared custody until a home study could be done. This meant that a child welfare investigator would be coming to dig through Tiphani's life, asking her all types of personal questions and questioning whether she was a fit parent.

Derek had definitely not heard the last from her. She was now hell bent on getting her husband back for this. There wasn't much she could say in the courtroom. If she brought up any of the dirt she knew about Derek, she would easily have been implicated in all of his dirty-ass dealings as well. The one thing she could not afford was to be associated with Scar Johnson in any way.

She stormed from the courtroom and immediately dialed Scar's phone number. Normally, she would have been more cautious when contacting Scar, for fear that his phone was being traced, but at that moment, Tiphani was so angry she wasn't thinking straight.

When he picked up, she couldn't hold back her anger. "I need to see you right away. This bastard needs to be stopped," Tiphani gritted out.

"Meet me at our usual spot tomorrow," Scar said and hung up immediately. He, too, was paranoid about his conversations being taped.

Derek left court feeling vindicated. He was going to pull out all of the stops to make Tiphani and Scar suffer. Derek called his team and asked if everything was in place for later.

Derek got the answer he was looking for and smiled.

Later that night, Scar sat in his office feeding money stacks into his money machine. It was the only thing that made him feel better lately. Suddenly, he heard someone running outside the door to his office. Scar pulled his gun out and got ready.

"Yo, boss! We gotta get the fuck outta here! I just got word that all the spots in the east are getting hit right now! My phone is blowing up. All ten spots. Niggas said it's the DES, DEA, FBI, ICE—all those fuckin' pigs!" Scar's lieutenant reported, so out of breath he could barely get the words out.

Scar jumped up from his seat. He had to get the fuck out of his spot because he could not be sure if this was a coincidence or if Derek would be sending the feds to get his ass at his secret spot. Derek knew about Scar's secret spot, so it seemed logical that they would be coming.

Scar started stuffing his stacks of money into bags. He grabbed his weapon and raced out through the secret tunnel underneath Katrina's. As soon as he made it into his truck, he heard. "Police! Freeze! Police!"

The police had busted into his spot from every direction. Scar's other workers were being taken down. There was no time to think about them now. Scar and his right hand man pulled out through the back road. They had just missed the raid by the skin of their asses.

Scar's chest heaved in and out. He wanted to fuck something up. He started banging on the dashboard. He banged until his hands hurt. "I'm gonna murder his whole fuckin' department! They wanna fuck with Scar Johnson? This fuckin' government is responsible for all the foul shit that ever happened to me in my life! I am the fuckin' King of Baltimore! Those mu'fuckin' boys in blue about to be singing the Maryland blues!" Scar screamed at the top of his lungs, his ugly scarred face twisted into a hideous mug.

Back at the station house, Derek smiled and did a little dance as he got word that all of the raids on Scar's spots were successful. His unit had reported back to him that they were almost positive that out of the sixty corner boys and trap house bodies they had arrested, somebody would be willing to roll on Scar in a court of law for their own freedom.

Derek was overjoyed. This time there would be no mishap with the warrant. He couldn't contain his joy as he slapped five with his unit and excitedly asked for details. Derek could just picture how crazy Scar must have been going right then.

When his unit turned into the station house, Derek held a final out-brief with them and got all of the information he needed.

"That was a good fucking job today. I appreciate all of your hard work," Derek commended them.

"I'm going the hell home. This has been two weeks of long-ass days and nights and fuckin' crazy hours. I'll be back in the morning," Cassell announced, stretching his arms for emphasis.

"Yeah, me too," Bolden said, agreeing, standing up to follow Cassell out the door.

"Okay. Go home, recharge, and I will see you guys back here tomorrow," Derek said.

Derek, Archie, and Rodriquez were staying a bit longer to firm up some paperwork. They all watched the two officers leave the station house, happy to be going home to their families.

"What are you two going to do?" Derek asked Rodriguez and Archie. He wanted to go get drunk as hell—his new way to ease his pain.

"I'm about to get in my ride," Rodriguez started, but before the rest of her words could leave her mouth, *Boom!*

Derek and Archie jumped and ducked their heads down. The officers all looked at each other, puzzled. Rodriguez almost choked on her words. The noise, which sounded like an explosion, was coming from outside.

All three officers rushed to the station house doors. They first noticed Bolden's car on fire. "Oh, shit!" Rodriguez screamed. Just as they began scrambling outside to try to get Bolden out of the burning car—*Boom! Boom!*—two more explosions sounded, stopping them in their tracks.

"It's Chief Scott's and Cassell's!" Archie screamed, shielding his eyes from the bright light of the massive fires as he stumbled backward away from the danger.

"Oh, shit!" Rodriguez screamed again, falling to her knees.

Derek stood rooted to the ground with his mouth hanging open in shock.

"Go get the extinguishers!" Derek screamed, finally snapping into action. Derek didn't know what to do. He soon realized that a fire extinguisher wouldn't do anything for those firebombs.

"Get some fucking help! Call the bomb squad!" he screamed again, his voice as high-pitched as a woman's. Everyone inside the station house began scrambling. The cars had been rigged to blow up. Derek knew damn sure that he, Rodriguez, and Archie couldn't get into their rides, or no one else inside the station house, for that matter.

Derek stood frozen, staring at the flames. He knew right away why this was happening. While everything around him seemed to move in slow motion, he realized that if his brother could retaliate this fast and right under the nose of a whole police station, he was in a war with his brother that would only end with one of them dead.

Chapter 7

Nothing Is Fair in Love and War

"He's trying to take my kids away from me and destroy my career," Tiphani cried, her tears falling on Scar's thick, muscular shoulders. "I'll do anything to keep my kids. I can't let him do this to me. He has to be stopped," she cried even harder.

"I'm not gonna let him ruin you. I'll ruin him first. Matter of fact, we can ruin his ass together," Scar said, stroking her long hair.

Scar was playing his part. He figured enlisting Derek's wife onto his team to help get revenge was a good strategy. Scar knew that after Derek's last hit on him and his return hit, shit was going to get even more dangerous if he didn't come up with a plan. Tiphani played right into his hand. Scar knew she was the type of bitch that worried about what people thought of her. She had come from nothing, and being a lawyer made her feel like someone, so having her husband threaten her career and everything she worked hard for would cause her to do anything.

"I still care about him. I mean, he is my husband, but I needed sex. I can't live without it, and he . . . he just couldn't do for me what you could do for me," she continued, more tears flowing.

She was also using a strategy. Tiphani could not risk Derek revealing the name of the person she'd had an affair with. If anyone knew she slept with Scar, she would most definitely lose her law license, and her face would be plastered on every newspaper. She could see the headlines now: PROSECUTOR SLEEPS WITH NOTORIOUS DRUG DEALER—SHE WAS ON THE CASE.

"Look, I think I'm in love with you, baby. All we gotta do is stick together. This nigga is as good as done," Scar said, putting on his Academy Award–worthy sad face.

He wiped the tears from her cheeks. He knew just how to seal their deal. "Let me find out you a little nymphomaniac and you need a piece of the Scar," he whispered. Scar rolled over and thrust his tongue into her mouth deeply.

Tiphani opened her lips and welcomed his tongue into her mouth. She immediately felt herself heating up down below, and thoughts of her husband destroying her started to fade.

Scar wedged his way between her legs as he continued to kiss her. He could feel a slick sheen of her body's natural moisture on the inside of her thighs. Scar grabbed his coveted manhood and drove it roughly into her slippery hole.

Tiphani almost choked, it felt so good. A gasp got caught in her throat. "Oh, Scar," she was finally able to manage.

"Do . . . you . . . believe . . . in . . . me?" Scar grunted out as he banged into her flesh with no mercy.

Tiphani's eyes popped open. Scar had never been this rough with her.

"Yes!" she screamed, grabbing onto the bed sheets in an effort to keep him from banging her through the wall.

All of a sudden Scar stopped, grabbed her roughly and flipping her over onto her stomach. "I control everything and everybody," Scar growled, grabbing a handful of her hair.

Tiphani tried to scramble away, but Scar's grip was too powerful. He snatched her back under him, parted her ass cheeks, let a glob of spit fall from his mouth onto her ass, and mounted her roughly from behind.

"Agggghh!" Tiphani screamed out in a soprano that was a mixture of pleasure and pain.

Scar loved to hear her scream as he drove all ten inches of himself into her asshole. That had sealed their agreement to work together to get Derek out of their way.

Derek attended Chief Scott's memorial service first, then Cassell's. He looked around at both services and saw some of Scar's henchmen peppered throughout the crowd of mourners. He exchanged menacing glares with them to let them know he knew they were there, and that he wasn't scared of their punk asses. Derek knew shit was real in the field, though.

He was thinking night and day about his next strategy. He wanted to hit Scar where it hurt, but he knew that would take some time to put together. His unit had been put on modified duties because of the mental anguish they'd suffered from Cassell's death, and from just knowing that someone was trying to blow all of them up. Derek knew he couldn't take too long to hit Scar back or else he'd strike first.

"Detective Fuller, I'm Chief Hill. Newly assigned to Division One," a tall black man with salt-and-pepper hair said, extending his hand to Derek.

Derek lifted his head and furrowed his eyebrows. He was a little taken aback. There wasn't any talk about a newly appointed chief, and he definitely never expected a black man. Derek silently extended his hand.

"I hear that this hit on Scott and your officer might have something to do with some dealings you've had with Scar Johnson," the chief said suspiciously, wasting no time letting Derek know he was being watched.

"I don't have any dealing with Scar Johnson. I have spent my entire time in narcotics trying to bring Scar Johnson down," Derek said indignantly. The lie slipped from his mouth so fast and with so much ease he almost believed it himself.

Derek acted offended by the chief's accusatory tone, but all the while his heart was thundering in his chest. He didn't know how much this new chief knew, and that bugged Derek.

"Well, all I'm going to say is tread lightly and get your shit together. There will be no more officers killed on my watch because of what you either did or didn't do," Chief Hill gritted out, giving Derek an icy look that spoke volumes.

Derek wiped sweat from his head and stormed away. *Who the fuck is he coming up in here, trying to tell me what I did and didn't do? Fuck him too,* Derek thought, his hands shaking so badly he had to put them into his pockets.

Even though he might not have wanted to admit it, Derek was shaken from the conversation. The pressure was mounting. He had to take Scar down before anyone found out about the shit his narcotics unit was into. His uneasy feeling from before was starting to creep back into his thoughts.

Rodriguez walked over to Derek. "What was that all about?"

"Nothing. New chief introducing himself. Wants me to turn the heat up on the Scar Johnson case," Derek lied, pulling himself together.

"Really? He wanted to fuckin' talk about work at a time like this? Fucking asshole," Rodriguez said, looking over at the new chief and shaking her head.

"Yeah. Seems like an asshole already," Derek said in a low voice, hoping he had convinced Rodriguez to stay on his side and help him get back to work against Scar.

***

After the service and burial, Derek left the cemetery alone—or so he thought. Derek was so caught up with everything going on and trying to figure out what the new chief was talking about that he didn't notice the person trailing him throughout the service and then to the bar after the burial.

Seeing the old dude with salt-and-pepper hair talking to Derek was a surprise to the observer. It was the same old guy that had been in front of Scar's mansion. *That old dude is the chief. I knew I recognized his ass from somewhere. Nigga be a cop! This is going to play out nicely. Scar, the chief, and Detective Fuller are all in it together. Time to play these fools like marionettes.* The shadow couldn't have been any happier.

It had been an emotional and fucked up couple of days, and returning to Rodriguez's house, all Derek wanted to do was get some much needed rest. When he walked in, Rodriguez was waiting for him.

"This was left here for you," Rodriguez said, tossing a manila envelope to Derek.

"What's this?" Derek asked angrily.

"I don't know. Someone rang my doorbell and left it."

"Who was it?"

"Don't know. They were walking away by the time I got to the door. I only saw the back of her. I'm assuming it was your wife."

Rodriguez was happy to let Fuller stay at her house, but she wasn't happy that his crazy wife was leaving envelopes on her doorstep, or, for that matter, that she knew Derek was staying there. If Fuller wasn't still married to the tramp, Rodriguez would have run after her and beat that bitch to a pulp.

"Fuck that bitch!" Derek spat, grabbing the envelope and tearing it open.

Rodriguez looked on curiously, wanting to see what was in the envelope. While she waited for Derek to arrive, she had started to open it, but although the curiosity was killing her, she decided against it.

Derek almost fainted when he pulled out the contents of the envelope. He looked up at Rodriguez with wide eyes.

"What is it, Derek?" Rodriguez asked, walking toward him.

Trembling all over, Derek placed the contents up against his chest to hide it. "It's nothing. This bitch thought sending me naked pictures of herself was going to get me back," Derek fabricated on the spot, thinking quick on his feet. His heart was beating like crazy. His stomach muscles were tightend, and he felt like he'd shit on himself.

Speechless, Rodriguez looked at Derek curiously to gauge his reaction. To her, his wife had been a fool to cheat on him. Rodriguez had always been attracted to Fuller, ever since she had first met him, but knowing that he was married stopped her from expressing her interest.

"But doesn't she think that it's too little too late for all of that?" Rodriguez commented. She walked up behind him and put her hands on his tense shoulders as she began to rub them softly.

At first Derek was taken by surprise, but then he began to relax. Her hands felt good. A woman's touch felt good. He felt wanted.

"I mean, she didn't appreciate you when she had you," Rodriguez flirted. Her hands moved from his shoulders to his neck, and she reached up and rubbed his head. Rodriguez's heart raced as her pussy grew moist. She could feel her clit begging to be touched, and she felt the rise and fall of Derek's labored breathing.

"I'd appreciate you, Fuller," she whispered. She turned him around and looked up at him while her hands roamed his chest, now underneath his shirt.

He looked at her lustfully. Her Hispanic roots gave her a goddess-type body, and her long hair was down around her face. She only wore it that way in the comfort of her home, but it was a welcomed change from her usual sleek ponytail. She looked sexy, and for the first time, he remembered that Rodriguez was more than a cop. She was a woman.

"I've wanted you for a long time, Derek," she admitted, lust lacing her words. She reached up and pulled his face toward hers and put her tongue in his mouth.

He sucked it hungrily, kissing her deeply as he palmed her luscious ass and hips. His dick instantly rocked, and Rodriguez could feel it pressing against her flat stomach.

"I love you, Derek. I've watched and loved you for a while now," she admitted. "My pussy is so wet right now," she moaned as he ripped her blouse open, revealing beautiful D-cup breasts in a purple satin bra.

"Damn," he admired as he licked each mound, releasing her nipple and teasing it with his tongue. He was horny as fuck. He felt a fire in his loins like no other, and he mentally began to prepare himself for the sex to come. He had never seen Rodriguez with a man, or even heard her mention a boyfriend, so he knew her pussy was tight and ready. Sexing her would be a welcomed distraction. She made him feel wanted, and right now that was what Derek needed.

He stripped her, and she removed his clothes; then he picked up her petite frame and placed her directly on his dick, no rubber and no second thought.

She felt like heaven, and his dick filled her up nicely as she began to speak in Spanish while she bounced on his dick.

"Oh shit, Derek. Yes . . . fuck me! Fuck this pussy, papi!" she screamed.

His mojo was on point, until he began to think about what he was doing.

"Fuck me!" she moaned, but instead of hearing Rodriguez's voice, he heard his adoptive mother's, and just like all the times before, he nutted too quickly. Cumming after only five minutes of stroking, he pulled out of her and shot his fluid on her stomach.

Embarrassed, he stood quickly. "I'm sorry, Rodriguez."

"Derek, it's okay," she said sincerely as she stood up and reached for him. She didn't care that he had only lasted a short while. She didn't know it was a recurring problem; she just thought that his nerves had taken over from the fact that he was fucking a long time friend.

"I'm sorry. I just need to get my head together," he mumbled as he picked up his clothes and the envelope full of pictures, then rushed up the stairs to the bedroom Rodriguez had let him crash in.

Rodriguez ran her hands through her hair, unsure of what had just happened. She knew that she could not change it now, however, and hoped that she wouldn't come to regret showing her true feelings.

Derek scattered the pictures out on the bed. He bit into his bottom lip until he drew blood. There were pictures of Derek hanging with Scar and his crew, and pictures of Derek leaving Scar's club and house with duffel bags. There were also pictures of Derek with stacks of money in his hands as Scar handed them to him.

The most damaging picture was one Derek knew had known he would regret taking—him sitting behind Scar's desk, surrounded by stacks of money and bricks of cocaine. Scar had urged him to see how it felt to be a powerful drug kingpin for a minute. After a little coaxing and teasing from Scar, Derek reluctantly sat behind the desk. Scar's crew was so hyped that there was a detective sitting behind the desk they all pulled out their cell phones and started taking pictures and video. Derek had barked at the little flunkies to stop snapping pictures with their cell phones, but obviously it had been too late. In return, Scar asked Derek for his badge so Scar could see how it felt to be a cop for a minute. Again Derek was reluctant, but finally gave in. He let Scar take pictures with his gun and shield.

Now Derek could only blame himself for being so stupid and not trusting his instincts. He knew playing around with gangsters and taking pictures would come back to haunt him, but he didn't listen to his own conscience.

Derek grabbed up the pictures in a fury and began ripping them up. He took his gun out of his holster and put it in his mouth several times. He was seriously considering killing himself. There was no way he could risk the pictures coming out in the media. He would be fucked! Jail was not a place Derek was willing to go, especially over some shit like this.

Fuck that! Derek wasn't about to punk out and kill himself and let Scar win that easily. He had to make a move and make it fast. "Scar, you fucking piece of shit!" Derek growled.

As usual, Scar left out the back door of Derek and Tiphani's house. He had a smirk on his face, thinking about the serious pussy pounding he had just put on her ass. He also felt real good that she had done the deed of delivering a copy of his blackmail material to Derek. Scar knew Derek must've been shitting bricks after seeing those pictures. He figured his big brother should've known that he had video cameras everywhere that he could run back and make stills from.

Scar always had it in the back of his mind that shit would go sour with him and his brother one day. If truth be told, he had never really forgiven Derek or his mother for all of the torment he went through as a kid.

Scar walked through the neighbor's back-yards and came around to the front of the house two doors down. He looked around and started up the street to his truck. He never parked right in front of Tiphani and Derek's house.

As he ambled forward thinking about his next move, he heard footsteps thundering in his direction.

"Scar Johnson, freeze! Police!" they screamed out.

"Not this bullshit again," he mumbled. Scar was suddenly surrounded by a swarm of police officers with guns drawn. He stopped dead in his tracks and raised his hands. This was all too familiar, except this time it wasn't an acting job, nor did he know they were coming.

"Keep your hands up and turn around until I tell you to stop!" one of the cops screamed out.

Scar did as he was told. When he turned to face them—

"Gun!" they screamed out.

Since Derek had busted up on them before, Scar never went over there without being strapped.

"Yo, be easy. I'm not gonna try nothing funny," Scar yelled out, knowing that if he didn't, those quick-to-shoot-ass cops would've filled his ass full of lead.

"Get on ya fuckin' knees and keep ya hands up!" an officer screamed out. Scar did as he was told. He could hear an officer approaching from the back. About sixteen others kept their guns trained on him, and he could see the glare from a red laser sight shining on his nose.

Scar suddenly felt a hand reach around the front of him and grab his gun out of his waist-band.

"I got it," the officer yelled as he retreated away from Scar.

"Take him down," another one screamed. Suddenly Scar was pushed face down on the ground. Three or four officers dropped knees into his back and roughly grabbed his arms and pulled them around his back.

"Stephon 'Scar' Johnson, you are under ar-rest, and here is the arrest warrant!" an officer said, placing the paper up to Scar's face as they pulled him up off the ground. "You have the right to remain silent, anything—"

"Yeah, yeah, mu'fucka, I've heard it all before," Scar grumbled. Once again he was forced into a police car. This time Scar had no idea what probable cause they had to be lock-ing him up. The only thing he could think of was that one of those weak-ass corner boys on his payroll must've been down at the station house singing like a fucking bird about Scar and his operation.

Scar flexed his jaw just thinking about it. Every time he felt he had gotten an upper hand on his brother, Derek came back with something else to bring him back to reality. This was a real war, and although he knew he would have to temporarily get someone to fight for him, Scar was willing to do anything now. Derek had to be stopped.

"Make sure I get a phone call to my fucking lawyer," Scar spat as the door to the police car slammed shut.

Chapter 8

Man Down

Derek smiled when he heard that they had picked up Scar on the arrest warrant; however, he wasn't too happy to know that Scar was picked up on the block where he used to live with his wife. The officers that had been following Scar to prepare for the arrest were all buzzing about Scar being on Derek's street. They had been unable to see exactly which house Scar had gone into, though, since they had stayed a few car lengths away. Scar had parked down the street and walked through a bunch of backyards and disappeared.

Derek knew immediately that Scar had been in his home fucking his wife again, and the idea of it incensed him. His imagination started to run wild. He was picturing Scar fucking Tiphani; then he could see Scar cooking breakfast in his kitchen and picking up his little girl or playing video games with his son.

Derek slammed his fist on his desk, garnering a few strange looks from other officers and staff members around him. Derek wanted to clear his mind. He had been plagued with crazy thoughts and ideations. Once, he had even seen himself strangling Tiphani until the life went out of her eyes.

Shaking his head and trying not to stress, Derek stood up to go outside for a bit of fresh air. When he turned around to leave his desk, he bumped head first into Chief Hill. *Fuck!* Derek screamed in his head.

"Excuse me," Derek said, startled.

"Were you responsible for the arrest of Scar Johnson today?" the chief asked dryly, hardly fazed by Derek's nervous body language.

"Nah, um . . . I mean, he was picked up based on probable cause based on information from a confidential informant that we developed after the raids," Derek stammered. He didn't fucking know why this chief unnerved him so badly, but it made him angry.

Derek didn't like the look the chief was giving him. Fuck it, he could admit it; he didn't like the chief at all.

The chief looked him up and down with a scowl on his face. "Do you mean reasonable suspicion, Officer Fuller?" Chief Hill said.

"Detective Fuller," Derek corrected him.

The chief ignored the correction. "I want to see the probable cause affidavit. I want to know everything about the informant too. I will not be embarrassed in a court of law. I'm hearing rumors already that the judges are agreeing that they will set bail for Johnson if he comes before them.

"This shit is starting to look like a fucking witch hunt now, Officer Fuller. You should've waited until you had concrete evidence of a crime. If Johnson walks again, shit might change for you. Like I said . . . Officer Fuller," Chief Hill said with finality. He turned his back and walked away before Derek could say anything in his own defense.

Suddenly the chief doubled back. "I hope all of this 'out for blood' shit you got going on with Johnson doesn't have anything to do with a certain affair and divorce," the chief commented.

Derek almost choked on his own saliva. "What?" Derek said in a low whisper, squinting his eyes with contempt.

"I'm just letting you know once again that there will be no bullshit on my watch," Chief Hill reminded Derek, leaving him standing there dumfounded.

***

Archie left the station house in a rush. It had been a long couple of weeks. Detective Fuller had been pushing them extremely hard to go after Scar Johnson, and then the deaths of Bolden and Cassell. Shit had been weighing hard on Archie's mind, even causing him nightmares. He wanted to get home—no, he needed to get home. Even the modified duty status didn't make shit better.

Finally making it outside, Archie revved up his motorcycle and used his foot to release the kickstand. He refused to drive his vehicle after the car bombings, and he checked and doubled checked his bike each time he was ready to ride it. Archie was super paranoid at home, too, and forbid his wife from driving any of their vehicles either.

With his mind heavy, Archie sped out of the station house parking lot and turned onto the street, heading for home. He made a left, and so did the car that was following him. Archie made a right; the car turned right as well. Archie was oblivious to the fact that he was being followed.

He never usually followed the rules of the road, and often cut in and out of traffic to bypass cars when he rode his motorcycle. After the deaths of his coworkers, he had an over-whelming fear of dying, so he began to follow the rules of the road.

Archie stopped at a red light and placed his feet on the ground to steady his bike. He flexed his back and wrists, which tended to get a little stiff when he rode for long distances. Staring straight ahead, he never saw the black van pull behind him and the bodies dressed in all black approaching him from either side. A lady blew her horn, trying to warn him, but a gun was put in her face.

The light turned green, and just as Archie lifted his feet back onto the bike's gear ped-als, he felt something slam into the side of his head. He was hit with such force that he and his bike toppled over.

Archie opened his mouth, but no sound came out. He didn't even have time to fight or go for his weapon. A black bag was placed over his head, and he was dragged from under his bike, which had fallen on his legs.

Finally realizing he was in danger, he began to thrash and fight. Archie fought for air as his captors held him in a severely tight headlock.

"Mmmm," Archie groaned, his air sup-ply being cut off. Swinging his arms and legs wildly, he tried to fight for his life. He was thrown into the back of a van, while his bike was left revving on the street.

Scar was laughing as the judge set his bail at ten thousand dollars. He thought he had to be the luckiest fuck in Baltimore. Either that or his payoffs were paying off. Ten grand was candy money to him.

Scar had his lieutenant pick him up and post the bail. On the ride from the jail, he was filled in on the latest war move. Scar was happy to hear about the capture of Archie. He knew this would be a low blow to Derek and the Maryland State Police. Another one of their men missing would definitely start ringing some alarms and bringing heat on Derek's dirty ass.

They drove to a secret spot near the beach in Baltimore that hardly anyone knew about, even members of Scar's own crew. Scar rushed inside to ensure he wasn't spotted.

"Where is he?" Scar asked.

Scar was led down into an old industrial wine cellar, and there he was. "Well, well, well. Looks like your boss let you down," Scar said, looking at Archie's battered and bruised naked body tied to a chair. "So, I heard you won't tell my little friends here who the informant was that snitched on me after the raids," Scar said, lifting Archie's downturned head so he could look into his battered eyes.

Archie's eyes were almost swollen shut. They were riddled with blue, red, and purple bruises, and blood was crusted all over his face.

"F . . . fuck you," Archie groaned out, barely able to get the words out. Archie knew he was going to die anyway, so he wasn't going to go out like a bitch and tell Scar what he wanted to hear. Once Scar's little henchmen had taken the bag off of Archie's head and showed their faces, Archie knew he would never leave there alive.

"Fuck me? Aw, that's just too bad. You and your little crew have been trying to fuck me for years, but guess what? Your precious leader, Detective Fuller, is really Derek Johnson—my fuckin' brother—and he has been on my payroll for years. So, all of your hard work would've never paid off anyway. He fucked you!" Scar said, lifting his gorilla fist and punching Archie across the face for emphasis.

Archie didn't even scream. He was so numb from the pain.

"Take care of him," Scar instructed, leaving Archie to the wolves. One of Scar's henchmen walked over, placed the jumper cables on Archie's two big toes, and sent enough of an electric surge through his body to restart a car battery.

Archie screamed so hard and so loud that the back of his throat began to bleed. He knew he was better off dead.

Derek was sitting in Rodriguez's home, drowning his sorrows in a bottle of Hennessy when he heard commotion downstairs. Startled, he stood up on wobbly legs and pulled out his weapon to investigate.

Creeping into the hallway, gripping his gun tightly, Derek slurred, "Who the fuck is it?" He lifted his gun up haphazardly. "Rodriguez? You better say something before you get a few in your ass," Derek continued, his words choppy.

Stumbling on the stairs, Derek finally made it downstairs without falling on his face. Looking around, he started flicking on lights. "Who the fuck is in here?" he belted out, but he didn't see anyone in the house. He stumbled into the kitchen—nothing. It was the same result in the living room.

"Better had gotten the fuck outta here," he mumbled, walking over to the big bay window in the living room.

Derek pulled back the curtains on the window to continue his investigation, but he didn't see anyone on the porch either. Derek squinted and ducked his head to get a better view outside. He looked out into the street. He knew it wasn't raining, but he could see something dripping from the sky onto his car. It was like it was raining in one spot—on his car.

Out of the corner of his eye he saw movement. Maybe someone running away from the house? He couldn't tell; he was having trouble focusing. "What the fuck is that?" he spoke to himself, squinting harder. Finally, he unlatched the front door and stumbled down the front steps to the curb where his car was parked.

Gun in hand, Derek stood in the street in front of the hood of his car. Then he felt drops on his head too. Derek touched the liquid substance that was dripping on his car and then on his head. He looked at his hand and saw that it was covered in blood. "What the fu—" Derek slowly raised his head and looked up. He screamed, dropping his weapon and stumbling over the curb.

"Arrggghhh!" he screamed again as he looked up at the eviscerated remains of his unit member Archie. The sight of the blood and hanging intestines and guts caused Derek to pass out.

Scar's mystery stalker had been following him for weeks now, and this was the most gruesome thing the stalker had witnessed. The stalker had watched as Scar's henchmen took a beaten and bloodied body and strung it up outside of Detective Rodriguez's house. After the henchmen left, the stalker waited a few minutes before going to examine the body. The men had placed something in the pants pocket of the body and taken something out and thrown it onto the lawn. The stalker needed to find out what it was and who the body was. The war between Detective Fuller and Scar was in full swing, and there wasn't much for the stalker to do except make sure it went on long enough for both men to be destroyed.

As the stalker slowly snuck up on the crime scene, it became obvious that it was even more gruesome than it appeared from a distance. The body was strung up, gutted, and draining blood like a pig in a slaughter house. It was enough to send shivers down anyone's spine. Sure, the stalker had witnessed deaths and beatings before, but never anything so vicious. There was a split second where the stalker just wanted to turn around, leave, and forget about the mission. Hopefully Detective Fuller and Scar would just destroy themselves. But the stalker's obsession with payback and vengeance quickly put those thoughts to rest.

The first thing that was noticed were two big knots of bills, one in each front pocket of the body. The stalker took one, but it felt kind of damp, so the stalker thought better of taking the second one. It was left in Archie's pocket.

Next up was to investigate what was thrown on the lawn. It wasn't easy to see in the dark, so it took a while to find what had been thrown. Just as the stalker was about to stop looking and leave, the object was spotted. It was a cell phone. The stalker knew this could be beneficial to the one-sided war being waged against Scar and Detective Fuller.

Immediately, the phone was opened up and the contents were searched. There wasn't much on the phone that would help. Dejected, the stalker was about to put the phone away, but then a plan materialized.

It happened when searching through the contact list on the phone. Detective Fuller's name and number were on the list. The stalker first dialed Scar's number and hung up immediately, then repeated the action, but with Detective Fuller's number.

Just as the calls were finished, the curtains in the bay window were pushed open, startling the stalker. Immediately, the stalker wiped the phone of fingerprints and ran. During the retreat, the phone was thrown under Detective Fuller's car so it would be easier for the cops to find.

About five minutes later, the police received an anonymous tip about a dead body hanging from a utility pole.

The lights and sirens flashed around Derek as he lay knocked out. When Derek came back into consciousness, he was on a stretcher surrounded by EMTs and a swarm of police. Derek recognized more than one of the crime scene investigators.

"Derek? What the fuck happened here?" Rodriguez asked when she noticed Derek had opened his eyes. Rodriguez had had enough. She wanted an explanation, and was starting to grow very suspicious about the deaths of her fellow unit members and Derek's strange behavior. It seemed to Rodriguez that each time shit went down, Derek was nearby, or had just been in contact with the officer before he was killed. Both she and Fuller had been involved in some shady shit before, but never would she have thought about killing one of her unit members. To her, that was the grimiest and most low-down things anyone could do. She didn't want to believe that Fuller could do something like that, but everything was pointing that way.

She also had reason to believe that Derek had motive for killing Cassell. The day that woman dropped off the envelope for Derek at her doorstep, there was also a note left for her. It simply stated *Detective Fuller had a reason to kill Cassell. Check the warrant*. At the time, she ignored it, thinking it was just his wife trying to stir some shit. Now she wasn't so sure.

"I don't know. I heard a noise . . . I think I came down . . . I don't remember," Derek said groggily. He was dazed and confused. The mixture of Hennessy and the hit he took on the head when he fell wasn't helping.

"What the fuck you mean, you don't know? Archie is fuckin' gutted open like a pig, hanging from a utility pole in front of my house! Blood is all over your fucking car and your hands! What the fuck is going on?" Rodriguez screamed, demanding an answer from Derek.

"Whoa, whoa. Take it easy," an EMT said, stepping between Derek and Rodriguez. Derek just stared ahead. He was numb and in shock. He didn't have the answers that she was looking for—or at least he wasn't going to tell her. He was not the man she thought him to be.

"If you don't start giving me some answers and start trusting me, I want you to get your shit out of my fuckin' house! Obviously you're bad luck, Derek. Either that or you're a murderer, since the bodies keep piling up around you," Rodriguez said to Derek, then turned and stormed away with tears clouding her eyes.

Chief Hill approached Derek just as Rodriguez breezed by him. "Fuller, we need a statement from you, since you were on the scene when the body was discovered," Chief Hill said.

"I already said I can't fuckin' remember what happened! I had a few drinks, and I must've heard something. I don't know why I came outside, and I don't know what happened after I was out here, okay! I know Archie is fuckin' dead, but I don't know what the fuck happened!" Derek yelled, the vein in his head visible at his temple.

He was tired of everyone being up in his face, blaming him for shit. Maybe he had made the mistake of getting into some shit with his brother, but he definitely didn't have his own men killed.

"I don't know what type of shit you're into, Fuller, but you better get your shit together. I will not have another fuckin' casualty or a fuckin' war that you started over a bitch. And I better not find out you're a dirty fuckin' cop," Chief Hill said, pointing an accusatory finger in Derek's face.

His words hit Derek like a sledgehammer. *What does this mu'fucka know?* Derek asked himself. It seemed like the chief knew a lot.

"Hey, Chief! You need to see this," one of the forensic crime scene investigators called out to Chief Hill.

"Remember what the fuck I said, Fuller. Your chances have run the fuck out," Chief Hill said in a harsh whisper and disappeared.

Derek closed his eyes and lay back down on the gurney. He was wishing he was any one of his dead coworkers.

"Chief, look at this," the crime scene investigator said, showing the chief a rubber-banded stack of money sticking out of Archie's pants pocket. The money was covered in blood, so it made it almost impossible to see the denomination of the bills. The investigators took several pictures before removing the wad of money to place in the evidence collection bags.

"How much is it?" the chief asked as he watched. The investigator flipped through the bills quickly, careful not to contaminate the blood and DNA evidence. "Looks like it's about ten thousand or more," the investigator said.

"Why would an officer who is not even at top pay be carrying around that type of fucking money?" the chief asked quizzically. "Shit just doesn't make sense. Why hang the body here?" he murmured to himself.

"We got his cell phone!" another investigator called out as they scoured the street in front of the house. Chief Hill rushed over to where she had found the phone lying wedged into the sewer grate under Derek's car.

"Did it get wet?" the chief asked.

"Aside from a little bit of blood, I think we still got a good working phone," the investigator said.

"Turn it on," the chief demanded.

"Chief, I don't know if you want to disturb the evidence. It may cause us to lose something," she explained.

"No! Turn it on!" Chief Hill screamed.

She did as she was told. The chief snatched the phone from her hand and pressed the dial button to redial the last number called. The chief held the phone with a plastic glove over his hand and listened. It was ringing. Chief Hill was hoping that someone answered.

Just as he said that, Derek came limping over. "Hey, Grady, what ya got?" Derek asked the investigator that had found the money.

"Somebody worked him over really good before they gutted him like a Christmas pig," the investigator explained.

Derek shook his head in remorse. His phone began ringing. Derek fumbled with his pocket to get his phone out. He looked down at the screen. ARCHIE, it read. Derek crinkled his face and looked around.

He locked eyes with Chief Hill, who was walking in his direction, holding Archie's phone. Derek had a look of sheer terror on his face.

"Fuller, don't fucking move!" Chief Hill screamed as he handed Archie's phone back to the investigator.

Derek was dumbfounded. He had not re-membered receiving any calls from Archie last night. Why would Archie be calling him?

"Can you fucking explain to me why Officer Archie had ten thousand dollars of what appeared to be drug money in his fucking pocket, called you last, and ended up dead, strung up to a pole in front of the house you reside in?" Chief Hill asked accusingly.

"Wait one fucking minute. I don't know what you are insinuating, but you better back the fuck up. I've taken a lot of shit off of you in the past couple of weeks, but accusing me of having something to do with the death of one of my men is the last straw!" Derek barked.

"We'll see about that. As soon as the lab comes back with something, I will be seeing you. Until then, stay the fuck out of my way!" Chief Hill spat, leaving Derek with something to think about.

Chapter 9

Payback is a Big Bitch

Tiphani had been a nervous wreck with everything that was going on between her and Derek and Scar. She often felt torn between what was right, saving her marriage, and her love of Scar's dick. Now things were falling apart for Derek and definitely out of her control.

She had agreed to help Scar take her husband down because she was selfishly thinking about her career and how it would look if she lost custody of her children. Tiphani was at a real crossroads. She had just as much to lose as Derek. Taking her husband down might save her career and let her keep her kids, or it might cause him to open up a can of worms that would make her lose everything, including her freedom.

Right now she was having a hard time seeing a way out of this mess. She had backed
herself into a corner, and the only thing she
could do now was to put all her trust in Scar
and hope he knew what he was doing. Losing
her kids, her career, and her freedom were
definitely not an option.

With her mind heavy, Tiphani stepped onto
the elevator inside the state courthouse building, where she worked in the district attorney's
office. Being an assistant district attorney had
been one of her life's dreams. As a child, she
wanted to become a prosecutor so she could
rid the world of all of the men who committed
domestic violence and sexual molestation of
children—men like her father.

Tiphani had grown up in a home filled with
violence and pain. Her father was a serious
alcoholic who often beat her mother, sometimes so severely she would be unable to walk
or to see out of her eyes. Tiphani would watch
helplessly, making promises to herself that the
next time he did it, she would kill him and save
her mother. Each time the beatings happened,
however, Tiphani became paralyzed with fear,
unable to do anything except run and hide to
stay out of the path of her raging father.

When she would try to talk to her mother about it, her mother would make excuses for her husband and tell Tiphani that it was done because he loved her so much. Tiphani would say she wanted to kill him, and her mother would slap her for saying it and tell her to go to her room.

When Tiphani was fourteen, her father's abuse had finally taken its toll on her mother, and she suffered a brain aneurism and died instantly. Tiphani remembered thinking that although she would miss her mother, she was relieved that the poor woman would never experience pain at the hands of her demonic father again.

After her mother's death, Tiphani became like her father's wife instead of his daughter. She had to cook, clean, and basically take care of him like a woman would. Tiphani suffered in silence, constantly dreaming of the day she would leave home. The thoughts of killing her father were always there, but had been pushed to the back of her mind. Instead, Tiphani replaced those thoughts of murder with thoughts of revenge through her own success. She was determined to become a prosecutor and find a way to put her father behind bars legally. It was going to be her father behind bars for abuse, and not Tiphani behind bars for murder.

She struggled to stay on top of everything through high school and college, fighting to stay awake during class because she was so tired from all of the work she had to do at home. Due to the lack of love and affection at home, Tiphani was constantly seeking love from men. She would do almost anything to get the love she wasn't receiving at home.

Over time, she came to equate sex with love. So, in order to fill that void in her heart, she would sleep with any man that showed interest in her. Tiphani couldn't stop searching for that love, and sex was her addiction. If a man made her cum, she thought he loved her. Sex made her feel wanted and needed.

After Tiphani graduated from law school, her father died from cirrhosis of the liver, and, of course, left her nothing but his debt. Unable to keep the promise to herself to see her father behind bars, Tiphani found herself struggling to make ends meet with her entry law clerk salary. It could have crushed most women, but Tiphani was not going to let her father win, especially not from beyond the grave.

Determined to move up, make something of herself, and leave her abusive past behind,

Tiphani became the most driven budding attorney in Baltimore County. She would work extra hard, even when some of the white attorneys got over on her and took credit for her work. But Tiphani believed that cream always rose to the top, and that the people in charge would know and see that she was the one doing the best work.

Soon, the bosses did notice, and she began to make a name for herself and was asked to join the ranks of the district attorney's office.

When Tiphani met Derek, they had a lot in common. He was working hard to get to the top within the Maryland State Police, and he understood her need to overcome her past. Tiphani fell in love with Derek's charm. She thought he would make a great provider and family man.

The first time they had sex, she chalked up his misgivings to nerves, but she learned quickly that he couldn't meet her needs. Tiphani came up with a plan for herself. If Derek couldn't meet her needs, she would just make sure her needs were being met without Derek knowing. She was going to get some on the side. *Fuck it*, she thought. *Men do this shit all the time. Why can't I?*

There were some nights while they were dating when, after having their two-minute sex, Tiphani would put on her clothes, tell Derek she was going home, and go directly to a bar and pick up the biggest, sexiest guy there and fuck him in the parking lot.

After briefly dating, Derek proposed to Tiphani. She knew his sex was mediocre at best, but decided that she could try to look past it in order to have a good, trustworthy man who would take care of her. She would settle down and start a family and be a one-man woman.

Not even a year into their marriage, she was frustrated with their sex life and started to search for more dick to satisfy her needs. Tiphani did try to distract herself from her cravings for dick. She immersed herself into her work and continued her rise to the top of the ranks amongst her fellow prosecutors.

Her hard work caught the eye of the district attorney, and she began to get all of the high profile cases, even the ones her husband had worked. That was how much her bosses trusted her and her abilities.

As much as Tiphani needed sex, she never brought that part of her life into the workplace. That part of her life was for outside the office on her own time, without the prying eyes of her coworkers.

Snapping out of her reverie, Tiphani rushed out of the elevator, down the long corridor to her office. She could swear people were whispering and mumbling as she passed them, but she thought she was being paranoid. Finally reaching her office, she fished around in her pocketbook for her keys. She had her head down, and suddenly, the door swung open.

"Come on in, Mrs. Fuller," a man's voice boomed.

Tiphani was startled. She slowly walked into her office, and her jaw almost dropped to the floor.

"Good morning. You don't look so happy to see me," he said with a sinister grin on his face.

Caught off guard, Tiphani swallowed hard, trying to find her words. The fucking mayor of the city was in her office, waiting for her to come in. What part of the game was that?

Why the fuck is he in my office? What does he know? These were the first things that came to Tiphani's mind. She shuddered, a chill running down her spine.

"Ahem." She cleared her throat, trying to compose herself "It is . . . I mean . . . it is not every day the average Joe like me walks into her office and finds the mayor of Baltimore sitting behind her desk," Tiphani stammered, her words feeling like marbles stuck in her throat. A hot feeling rose from her chest, up her neck, and flashed on her face. She looked around, unable to move or speak. Tiphani was very familiar with the mayor, but having him right there, right now, was not what she was expecting.

Tiphani was surrounded. Mayor Mathias Steele, a slick-talking Southerner who would probably throw his mother from a train to keep his job, was in her office, along with her boss, District Attorney Anthony Gill, another self-serving character driven by a name and the possibility of fame. Tiphani felt like she'd walked into a bear trap, or like she was being ambushed by AK-47s and all she had was a butter knife to defend herself. Her body broke out in a cold sweat, with fine beads lining up at her hairline, threatening to take a dip down her face at any minute.

What the fuck do they want? How much do they know? The questions kept running through her muddled mind.

"Sit down, Mrs. Fuller. We need to speak with you about a serious matter that cannot wait," Mayor Steele said, leaning forward and folding his hands together on Tiphani's desk like it belonged to him.

Stay calm, stay calm, Tiphani kept telling herself. *They can't tie you to any of this shit storm.*

Tiphani looked at the mayor and immediately pictured him naked, and it wasn't because she was trying to calm herself down. She quickly closed her eyes to get the image to go away. When she opened them back up, Anthony Gill shot her an evil look. Tiphani knew he was probably really shitting bricks inside. Her boss hated to think he or any of his staff were in trouble or had brought negative attention to his office; but a personal visit from the mayor was a sure way to know that somebody's ass was in hot water.

Tiphani sat on the small black leather couch situated directly across from her desk. It was the same couch she usually had victims sit on to give her their story; or sometimes, defense attorneys sat there to convince her to plead their clients' cases out.

When she sat down, the leather on the couch made a noise, causing an ominous feeling to overwhelm her. Tiphani looked over the mayor's head at the wall where a large framed picture of her, Derek, and the kids hung. She swallowed the golf ball-sized lump in her throat and tried to be cool.

"Mrs. Fuller, I'm here because, as you may already know, your husband and his cohorts at the State Police Division One are being investigated. It has come to my attention that it seems Mr. Fuller is the ringleader of a group of dirty cops. We are finding out that he is into some high profile criminal activity. I'm not talking stealing evidence money from drug dealers or planting evidence, either. This is serious shit, Mrs. Fuller . . . serious, serious shit," Mayor Steele said, looking at her to gauge her reaction.

Tiphani stayed calm, although her heart thundered against her chest bone almost painfully. It was pounding so hard, Tiphani was surprised that no one in the room could hear it. Mayor Steele looked at her seriously. He wasn't there to undress her with his eyes like he usually did. Thoughts of the sexual trysts they used to have when she was trying to vie for her position didn't even come into his mind. He was there strictly for business.

"Tiphani, I understand that you may have some information to help the state's case against your husband. Is that true?" Mayor Steele asked, throwing one of those fishing questions at Tiphani to see if she'd bite.

She knew this game all too well, and was not about to take the bait. She looked into his hazy gray eyes and at his newly receding hairline. Biting down into her jaw, Tiphani prepared herself for the performance she was about to give.

"I have no idea what you're speaking about. As far as I was concerned, up until just a day or so ago when I heard about Officer Archie's death and that Derek may somehow be involved, I thought of my husband as a fine, upstanding citizen and a damned good police officer," Tiphani said, folding her arms across her chest. She knew she had to play the role of surprised or offended, because she was not about to tell the mayor and the fucking district attorney that she knew her husband was a dirty-ass cop and that the biggest drug kingpin in Baltimore County was his brother.

"Mrs. Fuller, I'm here to let you know that if you had even an inkling of what your husband was into, you'd better start talking and cooperating here and now. It won't benefit you one bit if we find out on our own," Mayor Steele emphasized, clicking his teeth. It was a habit he had that Tiphani now remembered she hated when they used to fuck.

"With all due respect, Mayor, you know me and you know my work in the past. I am a law abiding citizen, and I took an oath to uphold the law when I became a prosecutor. I did not know anything about Derek's dealings. In fact, I'm just as surprised by your presence here as you are by my obliviousness to his activities," she said coldly. Tiphani had put her game face on, and when she did that, she could be just as shrewd as any high-level government official.

Anthony Gill cleared his throat. "Tiphani, just so you are aware, the mayor and I have discussed this issue ad nauseum, and we have decided that we are going to bring any and all charges against your husband that will stick in a court of law. He will be prosecuted to the full extent of the law. We are not showing him any mercy. What he did was despicable. Like you and me, he also took an oath to uphold the law, and because of his selfish and disgusting ways, three police officers and a fucking police chief are dead!" Anthony boomed, his voice picking up bass as he spoke.

Tiphani did not flinch. She kept a stony poker face and tried to stand her ground. All kinds of feelings were ripping through her. Tiphani was confused, torn between the reality of her failing marriage, which was her fault, and a potentially deadly deal she had entered into with Scar Johnson—and now this potential maelstrom was brewing.

The room seemed to be spinning around her. Tiphani felt hot, and her stomach muscles began to clench. *Do I lie and risk them finding out? Or do I tell the truth and have them lock me the fuck up right here and now?* She opted to stand behind her lie that she knew nothing about Derek's dealings with Scar.

Tiphani thought about Derek and about some of the underhanded things he had done in the name of loving and protecting his brother. She thought of how hard Derek had worked to make their marriage a success, and she immediately felt a pang of guilt. But there was no turning back now. She knew that the shit Scar had planted around to make Derek look guilty was surely going to put Derek behind bars for life. It was time for her to look out for number one. She couldn't afford to feel sorry for the man who was trying to take her kids and her life away from her.

"Mrs. Fuller, this case is as high profile as it gets here. The exposure of a ring of dirty cops in bed with a drug kingpin suspected of killing cops and government officials is a dead winner for this office, and under my watch, it will assure me a win in the upcoming elections. It is what everyone needs around here to recover from the failed attempt at bringing Scar Johnson down. Now we have someone to blame for that cluster fuck," Mayor Steele spoke, his pale white face filling with blood as he got excited about the coverage a case like this would garner for him.

Tiphani didn't understand why they were telling her their plans for destroying her husband. She just listened intently, waiting for them to drop the bomb on her.

"Tiphani, we know you are senior assistant district attorney here, but you will not be on this case," the mayor announced, dropping what felt, to Tiphani, like an atomic bomb on her.

Tiphani felt like he had slapped her across the face with an open hand. Her cheeks flamed over and her head began to throb at the base of her neck. Before she could speak, he continued.

"It's a conflict of interest, for one, and I just don't think you'll be able to separate your feelings enough. Although I think you are the most talented body Anthony has in this office, I'm taking you off of this, and as a matter of fact, I don't even want you to attend your husband's trial," Mayor Steele continued.

He might as well have fired her, as far as she was concerned. With everything that this case entailed, Tiphani knew it was going to be a high profile case, which meant she wanted to be on it. She wanted name recognition, just like the rest of them. It also didn't hurt that if she stayed close to this case, she could make sure that no one would find out about her connection to Scar.

"Ashley Simms is going to prosecute this case. She is the only other halfway capable assistant district attorney Anthony has in this office," the mayor announced.

Tiphani almost fell on the floor with shock. She was livid. Anthony knew goddamn well that Tiphani and Ashley hated each other. They had been each others' fiercest competitors in the office. She felt betrayed by Anthony Gill and the mayor.

"Derek being my husband didn't matter when I was working cases with him and making this office shine like the brightest star in the state, did it? What changed now? Do you really think I'm that emotional that I won't be able to separate my feelings? I'm disappointed that you and Anthony view me as that weak," Tiphani replied, shaking her head and halfway pouting. She was floored.

Not that bitch Ashley. She will definitely think she won my top spot in the office now. That bitch can't hold a match to me, Tiphani was thinking as she tried to put a hold on her feelings in front of these two white boys.

"Look, we can't afford one mistake on this case. We damn sure can't afford Derek's defense attorney standing up in court, pointing out the obvious conflict of interest and the fact that you may have some culpability in his crimes. No way!" Mayor Steele told her. He was seriously not budging on the issue.

Tired and feeling browbeaten, Tiphani just acquiesced. She nodded her head in understanding and just remained quiet. Anthony Gill hadn't even tried to advocate for her, and Tiphani felt he knew exactly what the hell he was doing when he assigned the case to Ashley. Tiphani always felt Anthony might've been fucking Ashley anyway.

Weak-ass punk mu'fucka! Tiphani screamed in her head, shooting daggers at Anthony with her eyes.

"Mrs. Fuller," Mayor Steele began, standing up from Tiphani's desk and starting to make his way to the door, "I hope you understand what we are doing here and why. I just want to remind you that if I so much as get a sniff, one iota, so much as a fucking tick's dick worth of a hint that you had full knowledge, or even partial knowledge of your husband's dealings with Scar Johnson and the Dirty Money Crew, I will have your ass on a roasting stick in the same court of law you prosecute criminals like your husband in every day." He smiled at her evilly.

Tiphani felt like hawking up the biggest wad of spit she could muster and spewing it in his face, but she remained cool, knowing that shit could be worse. They could know about her and Scar, which would fuck her out of the game.

"Do what you have to, Mayor, but I'm a woman of dignity and my word. You of all people should know that," she said sarcastically, giving the mayor something to think about.

His face turned bright pink and he adjusted his tie. He broke eye contact with her, clearly uncomfortable. Without another word, Mayor Steele sped from her office, with little flunky-ass Anthony Gill on his heels.

"Punk-ass bastard," Tiphani mumbled. She rushed around her office collecting files and certain things that she needed. Tiphani had planned to take some time off anyway. Between the family court proceedings and Derek's constant attacks, she was overwhelmed.

Tiphani picked up all of the files that she needed, checked her voice mail, and decided she would just leave the office. As she prepared to lock up, her cell phone rang. It was Scar. She picked up immediately.

"Yo, I need to see you now," Scar huffed into the phone.

"I can't right now. The fucking mayor just left my office," she whispered, looking around suspiciously to make sure no one was passing by and could overhear her.

"Get at me as soon as you leave there," Scar demanded, disconnecting the line. Tiphani pulled the phone down from her ear and looked at it in shock. He had hung up on her, and he didn't sound too happy.

Not more fucking drama from him now, she said to herself.

Feeling the weight of the world on her shoulder, Tiphani carried her stuff and loaded into the elevator, where some of her fellow prosecutors were already standing. Tiphani was sure they'd heard about what was going on with her, and that her arch nemesis was getting to move into her senior spot. She rolled her eyes, not wanting to deal with another fucking piece of drama right now. She gave them her back and didn't even acknowledge them.

Tiphani could feel them staring at her, and hear them trying to whisper about her. When the elevator reached the lobby Tiphani turned on them. "You know, if you put as much energy into trying to be half the prosecutor I am as you do into being in my fucking business, you might reach my level one day," she spat, turning and storming out of the elevator.

With everything that was on her mind, all she wanted to do was get into her car and go the fuck home. She didn't want to see or hear from Scar. She didn't want to see or hear from Derek. Alone time is what Tiphani longed for; time to process the day's and week's events and figure out what her next move would be.

Walking toward her car, Tiphani noticed a tow truck parked behind her. "Now I'm gonna get blocked in. What the fuck else could go wrong?" Tiphani mumbled to herself. Then as she got closer, she noticed that her damn car was rigged to the back of the tow truck.

"Hey! Hey!" she screamed out, dropping all of her files and running toward her car. The tow truck driver looked at her strangely. To him she looked like another crazed lady running at him. In his line of business, he had seen this same situation play out a million times.

"What the fuck are you doing?" Tiphani huffed out, finally getting to where her car was being hoisted onto its two front tires.

"What does it look like, lady? I'm repossessing this car, duh," the driver said sarcastically.

Tiphani looked at his little acne-ridden teenage face and had to restrain herself from slapping the shit out of him.

"Repossessing it? There must be some fucking mistake. I'm a fucking lawyer. You think I can't afford my goddamn car note?" she shot back, the heat of embarrassment settling on her face.

"That's what they all say, lady. Blah, blah, blah, I'm sure you can afford your car, but right here on this order I have, it says this car . . . Mercedes-Benz E550 that belongs to one Derek Fuller is to be repossessed today at the request of the owner, who has refused further payments to your lien holder. Repossession is to take place today, Miss. Not tomorrow, not next week—today. And that's what I'm fixing to do," the smart-mouth boy said.

"Let me see that shit!" she screamed, snatching the orders from his bony fingers. Sure enough, that bastard husband of hers had launched another missile at her. He had taken back the car he'd given her as a gift. That bastard was really trying to destroy her piece by piece—a low, painful take down.

Tiphani was seething inside. Her heart was about to explode, and tears burned at the backs of her eyes. Tiphani whirled around, feeling like all eyes were on her. She could see people stopping to look. Then she felt like dying when she spotted Ashley Simms and a bunch of the same coworkers she'd just told off looking and pointing. They were getting a kick out of her misery.

"Listen. Whatever the fees are, or whatever is owed, I will pay it. I have a bank account full of money. Trust me," Tiphani stammered, fumbling with her purse to get her checkbook.

"Miss, I can't even take your money if I wanted to. This car is not in your name, and I don't take bribes," the boy informed her.

"I can pay you more than that piece of shit job of yours could ever pay! Listen, you little shit, I need to get home. Now, if you don't take my fucking car off that rig, I will beat your ass right here and now," Tiphani barked. She had lost all sense of composure. It was not like her to come apart this way, but the ground was falling out from under her at this very minute. She was losing control of her life.

"Lady, if you want to go to jail, you can try that, but with all of these government folks watching, I don't think you will really do anything. Besides, you need to take this all up with this man, Derek Fuller, who I am assuming is your lover, boyfriend, or husband. Or you can simply call the car company and curse them out. But me, I'm just doing my regular nine to five job. Now, if you would move from in front of my truck, I would appreciate it." The boy climbed into the tow truck, leaving Tiphani standing there, looking like an ass.

She hung her head and tried to think of what her next move would be. All sorts of ideas were cramming into her brain at once; then something hit her like a bolt of lightning. There was only one way to solve this shit with Derek once and for fucking all.

Like a woman possessed, Tiphani stormed back toward the building.

"Show's over, bitches!" she screamed toward the growing crowd of coworkers that had been reveling in her undoing. Some of them laughed, some felt sorry for her, but Tiphani knew what all of them were thinking: How does a woman who was once at the top of her game, with everything you could dream of, suddenly lose it to the point of being looked at like one of the criminals she used to prosecute?

Inside the building, Tiphani pressed the elevator buttons with urgency. She planned to go back upstairs and give Anthony Gill a piece of her mind. Yes, she had stayed passive in their meeting with Mayor Steele, but she wasn't going to take this shit lying down. Derek was going to regret the day he was fucking born, much less the day his whack-dick ass crossed paths with her.

Tiphani paced the floor, thinking and waiting for the elevator. She rehearsed in her mind what she had to say to Anthony, and the fucking mayor, for that matter. The elevator doors opened with a dinging sound, and Tiphani went to rush inside. She bumped head first into Mayor Steele and his protective detail. Tiphani's chest was heaving and her hair was like a crazy bird's nest.

"Mayor, I need to speak with you," Tiphani said with urgency lacing her words.

"Mrs. Fuller, I think we've already discussed everything there is to discuss," the mayor said dismissively.

"I don't think so, Mathias," Tiphani said in a harsh whisper.

The mayor's eyes went squinty, resembling slits. He flexed his jaw and grabbed her arm, pulling her out of earshot of the officers in his detail.

"What the fuck are you doing?" he asked.

Tiphani had hit a nerve. She had always remained tight-lipped about their affair and all of the underhanded shit he did to become mayor. She had given him her word that if she was appointed as an assistant district attorney, she would never breathe a word of the things he was into or their little thing. Word getting out would make him seem like a philandering adulterer, and that would tarnish his chances of becoming governor.

"I am here to tell you that the fucking dirty cop case against my husband is the only chance I have left to try to put my fucking career back together and to be able to lift my head up with some dignity in this fucking town. I have worked extra fucking hard getting conviction after conviction to make you and Anthony look good! I have surpassed everyone is this god-forsaken place, and the thanks I get is being pulled off the case of the century! I need this like I need food right now!" Tiphani said, her eyes low with contempt and her voice serious as cancer.

"You will have Anthony put me on the fucking case right away, or else, so help me God, I will tell it all. I will release the pictures and the video," she gritted out in a harsh whisper.

Mayor Steele felt like he would faint. His head was swimming. The day they videotaped themselves fucking, the mayor knew he would come to regret it. He wished he had a gun. He would shoot this bitch right in her smart-ass mouth.

"You know that it will look bad if you prosecute the case, Tiphani. Why are you doing this?" he asked her, also whispering and looking around to make sure no one could hear them.

"I am doing what I have to do, Mathias. You and all of the fucking men in this county are trying to destroy me, when all I've ever done was work hard. Now I'm willing to work extra hard on this case, husband or not, but I am out to save myself. If Derek did something wrong and needs to be prosecuted, right now I'm the only bitch that can make it happen.

"You and I both fucking know Anthony is fucking Ashley, and that is the only reason why he assigned this to her incompetent ass," Tiphani said with passion in her words. She was up in the mayor's face, showing him that she wasn't about to back the fuck down. This was her last chance, and she needed this to work. She had to get on this case, and she would do anything to make it happen.

"But you think threatening me will work in your favor?" Mayor Steele said, trying to act like he would let her reveal their lewd love affair.

"Oh, Mr. Mayor, all you would have to do is try me. Either you have Anthony call me no later than nine o'clock tonight and tell me that by some miraculous act of God I am now assigned to the case, or I will be all over the media tomorrow morning, and your chances at being governor and mayor, for that matter, will be over," Tiphani said. She turned and began walking away. It was her way of letting the mayor know exactly who the fuck he was dealing with when it came to her. The same way they had trained her to be a shrewd, relentless bitch in the courtroom was the same way she'd turn on them and use it against them. Tiphani was a woman possessed, and she was hell bent on revenge right about now.

"Tiphani, wait!" Mayor Steele called at her back.

She stopped in her tracks, but did not immediately turn around. She waited a few seconds and then heard his footsteps approaching her. Tiphani turned around slowly, her face like a stone statue, hiding the real pain she was in.

"What is it, Mr. Mayor? How is it that I can help you?" she asked sarcastically, her voice cracking slightly.

Mayor Steele swallowed hard. He thought about all the times Tiphani had fucked him with a strap-on dildo and had him live out his fantasy of dressing like a woman during sex. He thought about how it would look in the papers, and what his little stuffy-ass wife would think. The images swarmed in his mind like a mini tornado, whipping his ass into submission.

"Tiphani, don't do this. You and I both know that a judge would never allow you to go on trial against the man you are currently in the process of divorcing. I know you are the best attorney we have, but keeping you off the case gives us our best chance at a conviction," Mayor Steele said in his smoothest, softest voice. The only thing he needed to do was get on his knees and it would have been outright begging.

"Yes, you're right, I am the best attorney you have, and no judge would allow me on a case with such a conflict of interest. But your best chance of a conviction is with me on the case. I can guarantee that. So, if you don't want the press to run front page stories about how the mayor loves women's clothes and strap-ons, you will find a judge and convince him that there is no conflict of interest and my divorce will not be admissible during trial." Tiphani knew she had the mayor in the palm of her hand, and she wasn't about to back down. Her life depended on it.

With his final attempt at changing Tiphani's mind failing tremendously, the mayor was backed into a corner: Risk bad press from losing a case, or risk even worse press for being outed as a sexual pervert. He chose the lesser of two evils in his mind.

"You are on the case. Get your shit together and bring your A game. I don't want to hear any excuses," he said with a worried look on his face. "Oh yeah, and get those divorce papers filed immediately," he continued, turning and rushing out of the building so fast that Tiphani couldn't even respond.

She smiled. Fuck it. If Derek wanted to play hardball with her, she would play the game. The only difference is she intended to win. Now she would officially be a part of Derek Fuller's downfall.

Chapter 10

Business Meeting

The Italian restaurant in Bowie, Maryland was Scar's favorite meeting spot. It was far enough away from the prying eyes of Baltimore to make it easy for Scar to conduct business undetected, but close enough that it didn't take up his entire day getting there. The layout was perfect for Scar to be able to see everyone coming and going, and at the same time give him the privacy that he needed.

As he sat with his eyes on the door and his back to the wall, he thought back to the first meeting he had there. Scar had come with his brother after Derek got his promotion to head the Narcotics Unit. From that point on, whenever they needed to exchange information and just catch up, this was the place they met. For obvious reasons, they had to be as low profile as possible. Being seen together would have been bad for business.

Thinking back, Scar couldn't believe all the ups and downs of his relationship with his brother. As he reminisced about the chain of events of their lives, Scar started to tear up a little. They had such a strong bond. They were a team, and nothing could keep them apart, not even the sheisty workers at the orphanage; but now they were so far apart nothing was going to bring them back together.

All because of some bitch, Scar thought to himself. With that thought, Scar immediately started obsessing over Tiphani. Yeah, he loved to fuck her and she would freak him whenever and wherever he wanted, but there were plenty of fish in the sea. Pussy was easy to come by, but having the brotherly bond that Scar and Derek had was sacred. Maybe if he took care of Tiphani, he could get his relationship with his brother back.

That's it. It's time to put this bitch to sleep, Scar thought as he started to hatch a plan to take out Tiphani. It would be perfect. Tiphani would be out of the way, Derek would get his kids back, and he and Scar could become the biggest players in all of Baltimore. He would also start planning a way to get Derek to become the next Chief of Police.

Just as scar was daydreaming about his future with his brother, the current police chief walked through the front door of the restaurant. Scar watched as Chief Hill stood and scanned the dining room, looking for the person he was there to meet. Instead of sitting at a table, the chief went to the bathroom.

What is this mu'fucka doing? Did he see me? Scar thought as he watched the chief enter the bathroom.

Thirty seconds later, Chief Hill exited the bathroom and sat down in the same booth as Scar.

"What the fuck are you doing?" Scar asked Chief Hill.

"Making sure we aren't being watched, and taking a leak," Chief Hill calmly said as he looked at the menu.

Derek wasn't the only one Scar would meet at the restaurant. Chief Hill was also one of Scar's insiders on the police force, and a frequent guest at the restaurant. They first started doing business together when Scar was just a young buck coming up in the game. Their careers had been linked and on the rise ever since. At first Scar just paid him to stay out of jail, but as his street cred and power grew, the amount of his payouts also grew, and he started asking for favors from the officer.

"What's so important that you needed to see me?" Scar started in immediately.

"Relax. Let me order first," Chief Hill said as he turned to get the waitress's attention.

"I ain't got time for bullshit. I got a business to run. The fuck is it you want?" Scar asked, his impatience obviously increasing.

Chief Hill just ignored Scar's last comment and called the waitress over. When she arrived, he ordered his meal and tried his best to chat her up. The poor girl just wanted to take his order and leave, but seeing as Scar always tipped her so well, she had to stay and endure Chief Hill's weak-ass game.

"Would you stop embarrassing yaself? Yo' game is weak," Scar said to Chief Hill as he turned to the waitress.

"Thank you, Lita. Just get my corny-ass friend his meal." With that, Scar handed Lita a twenty for her patience with Chief Hill and she walked away.

"Why do you always have to try and one up me? I was just having some fun. Is it so bad that I find the waitress attractive?" The chief defended himself.

"If you want pussy, go to a strip club. Shit, I own a few. Just let me know and I'll hook you up. Right now is not the time, though. There is some business that needs to be attended to," Scar said as he tried to move past the chit chat and get down to why he was there.

Chief Hill had reached out to Scar the day after Officer Archie was found strung up in front of Rodriguez's house. Scar knew that Derek was staying there, and he wanted to send a message to his brother. He also wanted the news to get wind of Archie being a dirty cop, so he planted twenty thousand dollars in Archie's pockets.

Scar was well aware of the power of the press, and knew how to manipulate them to his advantage. He was the master at anonymous phone calls to the newspapers, or making sure that TV news crews happened to be in the right place at the right time. He believed the saying that even bad press is good press. It was one thing he learned from studying the Mafia boss John Gotti.

Scar was feeling good that his message was being heard after his disposal of Officer Archie. The papers and TV all covered the story, with little hints about Archie possibly being a dirty cop. Derek's name was dragged into the story as well; although, with his newfound plan of reconciliation, Scar was kind of regretting that aspect of the story. So, when Scar received the urgent message from Chief Hill to meet him at the usual spot, he was not happy. His plan was to kill Archie, set him up, and then lay low for a while. Meeting the Chief of Police for an urgent meeting was not laying low.

"Shit don't seem too urgent the way you actin' right now. If you here to shake me down for some cash, you're sadly mistaken, nigga." When Scar called Chief Hill "nigga," you know his anger was about to redline.

"Okay, okay. Let's start over. It is urgent, and we need to discuss the matter of Officer Archie."

"I heard about that. I had nothing to do with that unfortunate event," Scar said with a knowing grin spreading across his face.

"I'm not here to ask if you had anything to do with it. I'm here to discuss the calls made by Officer Archie to you and Detective Fuller," Chief Hill clarified, knowing full well that Scar had everything to do with Archie's murder.

Scar's grin disappeared. He wasn't expecting to hear that. He had no idea what the chief was talking about. "Fuck you mean?" Scar asked.

Chief Hill now knew he had Scar's full attention. It was time to get down to a serious discussion and figure out how much he could trust Scar—if at all.

"I mean that there was a cell phone found at the crime scene. You know, the crime scene you had nothing to do with," he said sarcastically. "Well, on that cell phone there were two calls placed earlier in the evening. The first was to you, the last was to Detective Fuller. Do you know anything about that?"

The chief looked directly at Scar to see if he could read any of his body language. Scar stayed calm, but you could see in his eyes that his mind was working to sort out the information just given to him.

"So you say. How do I know you ain't lying?" Scar's first instinct was not to trust anyone. He figured this must be some sort of scam to get him to pay up.

"Why would I lie about this? The detectives on the case already know the last call was to Detective Fuller because when I recalled the number, the idiot was standing right there and answered his phone. They are having a harder time tracking your number, but it is only a matter of time before they figure it out."

"How the fuck he get my number?" Scar said out loud, more to himself than to the chief. "If this is true, so what? It ain't no thang. You just make sure they don't find out it's my number, and we all good," Scar said, trying to act nonchalant and put a positive spin on a fucked up situation. At the same time, he was basically telling Chief Hill to fix the mess.

"It isn't that simple. There is about to be a huge investigation into Detective Fuller, his unit, and the whole department. The bad press from this has gotten the mayor determined to put someone behind bars. There's an election coming up, and the mayor wants heads to roll. He is not about to lose because he looks soft on crime and his police force is completely corrupt," Chief Hill said, trying to explain the seriousness of the situation to Scar.

"A'ight, give me some time to figure some shit out. In the meantime, you keep an eye on the detectives and make sure they don't find out it's my number."

"You don't understand. We don't have time. The investigation is going full steam ahead. Once the mayor heard about the phone call to Detective Fuller and the ten thousand dollars in officer Archie's pocket, he is determined to close this case in a hurry," the chief stressed, reiterating the dire situation they were about to find themselves in.

"Hold up, hold up. Did you say ten thousand dollars?" Scar asked.

"Yes. Ten thousand dollars in his front pocket. The news is going to go crazy once they find out that a cop was walking around with that amount of cash."

"There was twenty thousand when we left. You tryin' to tell me that ten thousand just happen to went missing?" Scar said. This time it was his turn to stare and try to figure out body language. He was certain that Chief Hill was not telling the truth and probably stole the money himself.

"It doesn't matter. Ten, twenty, thirty . . . it's all the same. It was a lot of money for a cop to be holding. The main thing is I'm not about to let any of this somehow be directed back to me, so I need to know why Archie called you, and what kind of business you had with him." Now Chief Hill was getting visibly agitated.

Their actions were starting to attract a bit of attention, not what either of them wanted or needed. Most people just ignored them, not wanting to get involved in other people's business, but there was one person there who was very interested in what was going on. Scar's shadow was back, and paying full attention to the pair and their reactions. Although not close enough to hear, the shadow was still able to tell by the men's body language that the conversation was not an easy one.

After following Scar to the restaurant, the shadow was surprised, pleased, and intrigued by the fact that Chief Hill was there to meet with Scar. If only there was a way to be able to hear what they were saying. The shadow contemplated trying to get closer, but thought it best to stay away and not risk being spotted.

"We had no business. The only time I spoke to that nigga was when I was telling him to say his prayers before he was about to meet his maker. You best not be trying to pin anything on me. We're in this together," Scar said, letting Chief Hill know that if he went down, they both did.

"I know that we are in this together. I'm just saying don't try and fuck with me. We need to stick together. The investigation is moving forward, and Detective Fuller is about to go down. I just need to know what kind of business dealings you had with Officer Archie. I don't want any surprises coming at me during this investigation. The more I know, the easier it will be for me to steer the investigation."

"Away from you. You didn't finish the last sentence. Steer the investigation away from you. That's what you meant to say. You need to make sure you aren't involved. I hear what you're saying. You came here to warn me.

Well, let me tell you something. However I go, you go. Got it?" Scar warned.

"That's not what I meant. I came here to make sure we are on the same page. I am going to personally get involved with this case, and I need to know everything you know," Chief Hill said, trying to defuse the escalating argument.

"I've told you everything I know, which is nothing. Somehow you stole ten grand from me, and that pig Archie somehow had my number in his phone. That about sums it up. Let's agree to stay away from each other for a while." With that, Scar stood, preparing to leave.

"Agreed. One last bit of information, I would not trust that bitch D.A. you been fuckin'. Word is the mayor had a little sit down with her, and now she is on the warpath to clear her name. Watch your back," Chief Hill warned as he turned to the food that was just arriving at the table. "Won't you stay and eat with me?" he asked Scar sarcastically.

Scar was furious. Not only did he now have the chief to worry about, but he needed to keep his eye on Tiphani. To make matters even worse, his brother's head was now on the chopping block, and he didn't know if he could trust his own henchmen. If the chief was telling the truth, Scar didn't know who he could trust. He was becoming a solitary man, alone on an island, with no one to trust. Scar now knew that he needed to look out for himself and that his fantasy of reconciling with his brother was already not going to happen. The way it was starting to look to Scar, he was going to have to start playing everyone to make sure that he came out on top.

"Seems you already do most things solo. Eating alone won't hurt you," Scar said and walked straight out of the restaurant.

The shadow was dying to know what was said between the two men, but could only guess. Maybe with a little more time and trailing Scar, the answer would reveal itself. But for now, the shadow would just have to sit back and stay out of sight, orchestrating the downfall of Scar Johnson and Detective Fuller.

Chapter 11

Coming to a Head

Derek had stayed holed up in a hotel for two days, drinking himself into oblivion. On the third day, he finally decided to go to the station house to collect some of his things and let them know he would be taking some leave time without pay to get his mind right.

Derek pulled into the station house parking lot and noticed that the sign on his reserved spot had been removed and replaced. "Rodriguez? Hah! Ain't that a bitch? A nigga is gone for two days and the bitch he thought was his friend jumps into his grave," Derek said out loud. He knew that Rodriguez was hurt because he had never even mentioned their sexual encounter after it happened, but there was nothing to say. Derek had too much on his plate to stop and deal with a woman's problem.

He parked in a regular spot and went into the station house. All eyes were immediately on him when he walked in. "Hello to all of you mu'fuckas too," Derek said sarcastically, heading for his desk. Before he could even sit down for a second, Chief Hill was already standing over him.

"Fuller, I need to see you in my office, now," the chief said.

"Damn. Can I gather some of my shit first?" Derek asked, thrown off guard.

"No. You need to follow me now," the chief said with three uniformed officers flanking him, just in case Derek decided to act up.

Derek slammed the chair back into the wall as he stood up. He followed the chief to his office.

"Close the door," the chief instructed. Derek closed the door. His chest was heaving in and out. "Sit down," Chief Hill said.

"I'm 'aight. I'll stand," Derek said.

"Fuller, you are being placed on an indefinite leave until further notice. I'm sorry to tell you that you are under investigation for the murders of Archie, Bolden, Cassell, and Chief Scott," the chief said.

His words rang in Derek's ears like a fire alarm. Derek was too shocked to speak. After all he had done for the department, good and bad, he would never have had his men killed.

"You need to give me your gun and badge immediately and vacate the premises until further notice. You no longer have any police authority until, if, and when such time as you are sworn back in. Do you understand?" Chief Hill said.

Derek fought back tears. "I'm being framed. Can't you see that?" Derek croaked out. The chief just smirked.

Derek didn't know who to trust. Even his chief could have been on the take. He pulled his gun from his holster and placed it on the desk. He thought about blowing his own head off right there in the chief's office, but knew he didn't have the heart to kill himself. He also put his belt, badge, and credentials on the desk. Derek had been defined by his career for so many years that he already felt naked without his gun and shield.

"You and the entire Baltimore area will regret this. Scar Johnson will reign terror on you and the entire city, and I won't be here to stop him," Derek said, turning and storming out.

He stomped down the stairs and straight out of the station house. His mind was whizzing, and now that he didn't have so much to lose, he had a few people to pay a visit.

Derek went to his car, but was stopped before he could get in. "Excuse me, D," he heard a voice say. Derek spun around and looked at the person strangely. "I don't know if you remember me. I used to work for Scar," the boy said. His face looked kind of familiar, but Derek couldn't be sure.

"I'm Flip," he said.

"What the fuck you doing here, and what do you want?" Derek asked, angry at the intrusion.

"I want to help you set Scar up—not to go to jail, because he always beats the rap. I want him dead just as much as you do," Flip said, speaking like a little mechanical robot.

"Why should I help you?" Derek asked suspiciously.

"Because you and me are the only ones in this city that Scar don't got on his payroll. You see that fucking chief you got up in there? Oh yeah, he has partied with Scar many nights. One time, you and him had just missed each other coming in and out to get y'all payoff money. Believe me, you need somebody who knows all of his moves inside and out, from what he eats for breakfast to what time that nigga goes to bed. That somebody is me," Flip explained.

Derek looked him up and down. The boy looked injured and hungry. Derek didn't have shit to lose by just listening to this young boy's plan. "Get in," Derek said.

Rodriguez was overjoyed with her temporary promotion. She pulled into her driveway, smiling from ear to ear. When she got out, she noticed Tiphani standing at her door.

"Hey. Derek isn't here," Rodriguez told her shortly.

"I'm not here to see him. I'm here to see you," Tiphani said, motioning to someone in a car. Scar stepped out of his Escalade with its darkly tinted windows.

"Look, I don't know what the fuck is going on," Rodriguez started, putting her hand on her gun.

"It's not like that. We just want to talk to you," Tiphani assured. All she could think about was her looming family court date. She would be ready for her husband this time.

"Can we go inside?" Tiphani asked.

"No, I don't think that's a good idea," Rodriguez said nervously. She realized she was the only one left from the original Narcotics Unit that had taken Scar down.

"Will this give you some assurance?" Tiphani said, opening a bag filled with money. Lying on top was a picture of Derek and Scar, smiling, side by side with their arms around each other.

Rodriguez couldn't believe her eyes. She knew Derek was under investigation, but she didn't really want to believe it. When she saw the picture, she felt she had no choice but to listen. She hurriedly opened her front door and allowed Tiphani and Scar into her home.

Rodriguez moved away from them, never turning her back, and kept her hand on her gun. She was still not ready to fully trust Scar Johnson, Baltimore's most dangerous criminal.

"Listen, ma. If I wanted you dead, I wouldn't have any small talk. I would have blown your head off ten minutes ago," Scar said.

"What do you want from me?" Rodriguez asked with her hand still on her gun, unable to keep her eyes off the money bag.

"I guess you've figured out that your boss wasn't so clean. Well, we need to bring him down, all the way down for good, and we need your help," Scar explained.

"Shit, you got pictures of him with you. That's enough," Rodriguez said, growing angry. She felt she should've known Derek was dirty when that search warrant shit went down. She also felt like a fool because Derek hadn't trusted her with his secrets. They had both taken money from drug dealers in the past, but it never got to the point where any of the members of the unit were in danger of being killed—especially being killed by their own leader.

"No, it's not enough. You see, if Scar shows those pictures, Derek will just refute them. He will say Scar had them digitally made. He will say Scar is a liar. With Scar's reputation, whose credibility do you think will stand up in court?" Tiphani interjected, giving Rodriguez the lawyer-and-trial perspective on things.

"We need you to help us bring this dirty fuck down. Do it for your fallen friends. Do it for the good of the department," Scar said, trying to play on Rodriguez's morals. After waiting for her to respond and getting nothing, Scar then continued his mind games. "Better yet, do it for this," he said, dropping the bag of money at Rodriguez's feet.

"That's a half a million dollars in that bag. Nobody has to know if you just do what we need you to do. It's an easy decision. Your former unit members obviously didn't make the right decision."

Rodriguez looked like she was conflicted. That was money she could use, but that would make her no better than Detective Fuller. Rodriguez also knew that even though Scar was offering her this money for his help, he was basically telling her to get on board or she'd end up like Archie, Cassell, and Bolden.

Rodriguez's legs gave up on her, and she sat down on her couch as her thoughts went through her head a mile a minute.

Tiphani held her breath. She was counting on this last ditch attempt to amass something concrete on Derek. She needed this to work so she could distance herself so far away from Scar that no matter what Derek said, she would be safe.

"Why are you here? You working for Scar too? Why are you out to bring your own husband down?" Rodriguez asked Tiphani, suddenly realizing it didn't make sense for both of them to be there together.

Tiphani's lawyerly instincts took over, and she quickly responded to Rodriguez. "No, I am not working for Mr. Johnson. He is actually cooperating with the D.A.'s office to help bring in a crooked cop. As far as that crooked cop being my husband, it seems that I didn't know him as well as I thought. Because of my oath to uphold the law, I will prosecute anyone who breaks the law, even if it is my husband, and especially if that crooked cop has killed his own men." Tiphani threw in the last part to try to play on Rodriguez's loyalty to her fallen comrades.

"What do you need me to do?" Rodriguez asked. She felt like she didn't really have a choice but to get on board with Scar basically threatening her, and Tiphani making her realize that Derek probably killed his own unit because he was so entrenched in his own shit.

Tiphani smiled.

"You ain't gonna regret this shit. I can guarantee it. If shit works out, you can make enough money to retire from that fucked up place for life," Scar told her as he extended his hand for a shake.

Flip and Derek sat in Derek's hotel room, plotting. Flip drew a map of all of Scar's spots that Derek didn't know about. Flip told Derek the details of six murders Scar had ordered. He told Derek about stash spots where Scar hid money. He also provided Derek a long list of names of cops, lawyers, and government officials on Scar's payroll—one of which held a key position in the Baltimore mayor's office.

Derek shook his head. He would have had no wins against Scar no matter what he did, even if he was above board with his police work. Flip was all Derek had at this point, so he leaned in and hung on the boy's every word.

"Scar got this bitch name Julissa that does his hits for him. She is one bad bitch—beautiful, and she poses as a call girl, and then wham! She takes niggas out," Flip explained. "I heard she gets rid of the bodies by pouring battery acid on the shits until they disintegrate," he continued.

"I guess all this shit you telling me leaves us no choice but to kill the nigga," Derek said, looking off into the distance like he was spaced out. "Which means I'm gonna have to kill my wife, too, or else that bitch will be a prime witness," Derek said seriously. He couldn't believe that things had spiraled so far out of control. The two people that he had loved most in the world, he now hated.

"Hey, Travis," Rodriguez said, flashing her credentials to the little old cop who guarded their evidence cage. The man was one of those cops that just refused to retire, so they assigned his half-blind ass to guard the cage so he could sleep on the job if he wanted to.

"Hello, pretty lady. How have you been doing?" the old man asked. He was old as shit, but wasn't too old to pay attention when a beautiful woman was in his presence.

Rodriguez laughed to herself. She knew the old man said that to all of the female officers because he didn't remember anybody and simply wanted to be nice.

"I'm good, old man. I need to pull some evidence for one of my cases," Rodriguez lied.

"Sure. Anything for you," Travis said, buzzing the gate open for Rodriguez to enter.

Rodriguez rushed through and went into the cage where all of the crime scene evidence was housed. She looked up and down the rows, making sure no other cops or detectives were in there. When she was sure she was alone, she walked down the aisle looking for the letters.

"Right here, baby," she whispered. She yanked a large box off the shelf and pulled off the top. Inside, she stared at plastic and paper bags that were numbered and labeled. She sifted through them until she found what she was looking for. She picked up the piece of evidence and replaced it with a piece that had Derek's blood on it. Then she exchanged another piece of evidence with something that she had gotten from his house with Derek's

DNA on it. Next, it was Derek's fingerprints that she placed into the evidence.

"Done," she whispered, rushing to put shit back the way it was supposed to be.

Rodriguez walked back to the gate and noticed Travis was fast asleep. She buzzed herself out and never woke the old man.

Chief Hill watched the closed circuit security screen in his office. He let a small smile spread across his face. "Dumb little bitch. Did you really think this shit would be that easy?" Chief Hill whispered, rubbing his hands together.

Flip had given Derek a lot of information and a lot to think about. Derek was going to take this information and call some of his fed friends. The feds were notorious for putting hits out on dudes that they knew would keep beating the system. Derek had seen it over the years: from the Black Panther dudes to famous rappers, the feds would take a nigga out and make it look like black on black crime in a minute.

"A'ight, man. I will be in touch," Derek said to Flip, giving him five.

"Let me know what else I can do. I'm around. I wanna see that mu'fucka suffer for what he did to me," Flip said, holding up his hand and showing Derek his two missing fingers to make his point clear.

"I'll be in touch," Derek said. He closed the door behind Flip and pulled out his computer. It was time to make shit happen.

Flip stepped onto the elevator down to the lobby of the hotel. He felt good about what he had done. He got out of the elevator and walked through the lobby. As he stepped out of the hotel doors, he heard someone yell, "Yo, snitch!"

Before he could run . . . *Bang! Bang!* Two shots to the dome splattered his brains all over the sidewalk. The doorman ran into the hotel, screaming for help.

Tiphani called up the *Baltimore Sun* and anonymously reported where they could pick up a package regarding a big breaking news story. Then she called the detective assigned to the murder cases of Archie, Bolden, Cassell, and Chief Scott, and told him the same thing. The package was on its way, and what was inside would turn the city of Baltimore upside down.

Tiphani looked over the pictures again and reviewed the gun ballistics report that Rodriguez had given her. Tiphani couldn't help but smile when she read that bullets from Derek's personal weapon, which he had forgotten in their home safe, were found in the bodies of all the dead officers.

Tiphani called Scar. "It's done, baby. I made all of the calls. We will live happily ever after." She smiled as she spoke into the receiver. "I love you too," she said, closing her eyes.

Hanging up the telephone, she shrugged into her coat on her way to mail her packages. She grabbed her keys and stepped out her door. When she stepped down her first step, she was hit from the side. She wasn't able to scream before she was dragged away.

TO BE CONTINUED . . .

Coming Soon

Baltimore Chronicles
Volume 4

by Treasure Hernandez

CHAPTER 1

NEIGHBORS, WHO NEEDS THEM?

Scar's eyes popped open "These mu' fuckin' birds!" he had been woken up for the fifth day in a row by a flock of birds chirping outside his bedroom window.

"I hate the fuckin' country." He mumbled to himself.

He wiped his eyes and lumbered out of bed. The bright morning sun was shining through the south-facing window of his bedroom. He stood and looked out that same window at the blackbirds cawing in the tree. "I'm putting an end to this bullshit once and for all." Still groggy from his sleep he put on a pair of cream-colored sweat pants with a matching zip up top.

He had only been in the country house for a week but to him it felt like a year. He hated the slow pace and solitude. There was no action, no one around, and no fun. In short he was bored out of his mind. The first few days at the house were not so bad. He had been occupied by all the action of moving in. Being the head of the biggest drug cartel in Baltimore had it's advantages, he had some of his low level soldiers came out to move his shit while his top level soldiers sat down for a meeting about how things would run. Scar told them that Flex would be representing him in the city while he was stationed in the country. Although Flex hadn't been with Scar's crew for very long he showed loyalty and drive, the two things that Scar demanded. Scar noticed and rewarded Flex with a promotion. Scar felt that Flex had grown into a man. Especially the way he handled killing Sticks. Scar saw a definite change in Flex's demeanor after the young soldier got a taste of murder. So now, whatever Flex said was word. If any of them had a problem with Flex then they would have a problem with Scar. If Day had been at the house it would have been him who was representing Scar, but that nigga had disappeared and no one knew where he was. Since Scar had been in the country he hadn't seen or heard from Day. As a matter of fact, no one in his crew had. Finding out what happened to Day was one of the things on Scar's list. He just hadn't had much time to investigate since his sudden escape from Baltimore.

Fully awake now, Scar went to his closet and pulled out his AK-47. He inserted a magazine full of bullets and cocked the side handle. The machine gun was now loaded and waiting to inflict some serious damage. This was the last thing Scar wanted to be doing, but he had had enough. Every morning some damn birds were interrupting his sleep and he was sick of it.

The rest of the house was quiet as he walked out the front door into the early morning chill. He carefully and quietly walked around the house so he didn't alert the birds to his presence. They could be as loud as they wanted to be and Scar hoped they would be. He figured if they remained loud it would drown out any noise he would make and it would be easier to ambush them. "Enjoy your last chirps you squawking mu'fuckin' crows." He raised the machine gun, propped the butt end against his shoulder and aimed at the middle branches of the tree. A shower of bullets spit out of the gun barrel as Scar pulled the trigger. Bullet shells flew every which way and littered the ground. He sprayed the tree back and forth as the air filled with the smell of spent gunpowder. The black birds scattered and attempted to flee as they got bombarded with bullets. Some made it out and were able to fly away. Most got caught in the line of fire. Forced to stop shooting because the magazine was spent Scar dropped the gun to his side. He surveyed the damage he just inflicted. There were feathers and leaves still lingering in the air, taking their sweet time floating to the ground. They would settle next to the dead birds that had just been shot. Smoke from the gun barrel was swirling in and around the tree branches. There were at least twenty dead birds scattered around and lying in the grass. Scar was proud as he stood admiring his work. "Now maybe I can get some sleep." He stood on top of the hill and looked over the valley that sprawled out in front of him. There was only treetops and sky as far as he could see. It was the most isolated he had felt since escaping to the country. This lone-liness made him long for the good old days, when he was a youngin' and he and his brother Derek were inseparable. They looked out for one another. Even though they didn't have any parents and were in an orphanage they had each other. They were family. Scar longed for that bond again. He had it for a while until he started fucking Derek's wife Tiphani. That act of betrayal pushed Derek over the edge and de-stroyed any familial bond they once had. Now they were sworn enemies and Scar had no one close to him. He didn't trust anyone had kept everyone at arms length while becoming the biggest player in the game. Now he was starting to regret some of his decisions.

He stayed there for a good hour thinking about his past. He went over everything that had happened and all of his actions that brought him to this place right now. "Fuck that. What's done is done. Can't change nothin' now." He snapped back to the present and walked into the house. He wasn't about to let sentimentality get the better of him. There was a reason he was the head of the most notorious gang in Baltimore.

Scar walked in the house to his niece sitting at the kitchen table coloring in her coloring book and his nephew on the floor in the living room playing with his toy cars. The kids were too young to realize that they were being held as captives. Scar had taken them in order to get his brother Derek to follow his orders.

"Hi Uncle Scar." They said in unison as he walked through the door.

"What's up little ones? Why you up so early?" He hid the gun behind is back as best he could.

"We heard some loud bangs outside." His nephew said. He was the younger of the two children. "It sounded like firecrackers." Said Scar's niece.

"That's what it was. Firecrackers. I was trying to scare away the loud birds outside of my window." Scar replied. "Go upstairs and change out your PJ's and I'll make y'all some breakfast."

"Pancakes." Yelled his nephew.

"Pancakes." Scar smiled his crooked smile. Even though he had kidnapped the kids they were the only things that made Scar smile these days.

The kids raced up the stairs to see who could change the fastest. Scar followed them and put his machine gun back in the closet. Since they'd been with him, he had tried to hide the guns and drugs from them. He didn't want them growing up like he did. He wanted them to keep their innocence as long as they could.

Scar started mixing together the pancake batter and warming the griddle as the kids came rumbling down the stairs. "First!" His niece crashed into the table.

"Not fair you always win." Scar's nephew pouted.

"You'll win one day, big man. How bout you get the first pancake?" Scar tried to cheer the little man up.

Scar served breakfast as the kids occupied themselves with their own little games. They had formed a tight bond since all of the drama surrounding their family started. First their father Derek had been put in jail, then their mother Tiphani staged her own kidnapping and went away with Scar. Now their mother has disappeared and their uncle has kidnapped them. They had been shielded from it as much as possible but children are like dogs; they can sense when things aren't right. Kids are smarter than adults give them credit for.

"When is mom and dad coming to get us?" Asked the nephew.

Scar hesitated before he answered. "Soon, little man, soon."

"Maybe we should go back to Baltimore. They might not know where we are or they might get lost." His niece chimed in.

"I wish we could go back to Baltimore but this is home now. I talked to your pops the other day and he still busy. He'll get here as quick as he can." Scar lied.

"I don't like it here. I want to go back home." Said his nephew.

"Me too. Me too." Scar agreed.

A somber silence fell over the table, all of them sitting with their own thoughts. The kids thinking about their parents and wishing they were in their own house, and Scar wishing he was back on familiar ground, bangin' on the streets of Baltimore.

Scar was getting the uneasy feeling that he may be stuck in the country for a long time. If that was the case he needed to figure out what the hell he was going to do with the kids. He didn't want to become their father. When he kidnapped them he didn't think about keeping them long term. He was thinking about the present and what he needed to do right then at that moment. What the fuck did he know about raising kids? He couldn't look to his childhood as an example. He watched his mother get beaten to death and was in and out of foster homes his whole childhood. Not to mention having the state separate him and his brother while in foster care. He already felt like he was a father figure to some of these wild ass soldiers in his crew. He didn't need two real children to take care of and send off to school. Usually if Scar had a problem like this he would just kill whoever it was that was clinging to him. He was hoping to come to another solution before he had to do that.

The doorbell rang and snapped everyone out of their thoughts.

"I'll get it." Said the niece.

"No. You stay here." Scar instructed with a little force behind his words.

The kids obeyed and Scar quietly and cautiously walked to the front window. He carefully peeked out the window so as not to attract attention from whoever was at the door.

"Who the fuck?" Scar mumbled to himself.

He quietly walked back to the kitchen and told the kids to go play out back. They obeyed and went out the back door. Scar went into a cabinet and took out a 9 mm from the top shelf. He slipped it in his waistband as he walked back to the front door. As he approached, the stranger knocked on the door.

"Who is it?" Scar stood a little back and to the side of the door in case they started shooting or tried to kick the door in.

"Oh, hello. It's your neighbor." The stranger called back.

"Who?"

"Your neighbor Adam. I live just next door."

Scar looked out the window again to see if he could see anyone else. It looked to him like this dude was alone and he for sure looked harmless. After contemplating a moment Scar figured it was safe to open the door.

"Hello." Said Adam as the door opened to reveal Scar.

"What's up?" Scar replied to the white man wearing a wide brimmed straw hat and overalls.

"I just came over to say hello and welcome you to our community." Adam said. His warm smile formed his thin face into something out of a Norman Rockwell painting.

Scar was caught off guard by this unsolicited kindness. A neighbor coming over to introduce themselves would never happen in the hood.

"Oh. Word. That's cool."

"I brought you some vegetables from my garden. May I come in?" Adam handed Scar a wicker basket full of vegetables. Before Scar could react Adam had handed him the basket and walked into the house.

"I thought they would never sell this place. It's been vacant ever since Miss Sally passed away. Going on two years now. Oh, well guess that's the recession they are always going on about on the TV. I like what you've done with the place." Adam slowly walked around the living room.

"Yeah, well I was just getting ready to leave. So, nice meeting you." Scar was finally able to compose himself and say something.

"Oh, right. Of course. I'm so rude. I just got so excited when I saw that someone finally moved in I had to come over. I love having neighbors. I think of them as my family. Are you here alone?"

"Yeah it's just me." Scar held the wicker basket of vegetables.

"Oh well, you'll have to come over for dinner. I'm just over the other side of the tree line there." He pointed over to the east side of the house where the trees were the thickest.

"Yeah, maybe."

"I get it. You're shy. Well I won't bite. My wife and I own a small farm over there. Nothing fancy just enough to get by. We don't need much to be happy when we have each other." Adam smiled.

"Uh huh." Scar awkwardly smiled back. *What the fuck is this cracker talking about?* He thought to himself.

"You should stop by the farmers market this weekend. I sell my vegetables there on Saturdays and Sundays. It'd be a great way to get to know everyone in the community."

"Yeah, we'll see. I really gotta be going."

"Oh, right. I forgot. I'm sorry."

Just as Adam was starting to leave Scar's niece came into the living room. Adam stopped abruptly.

"Uncle Scar, there are a bunch of dead birds in the yard. Did the fireworks kill them?" She said.

"Yeah little one. That's what happened. Now go on back outside and play. Take these vegetables to the kitchen." He handed her the basket.

"Where did you get these?"

"This nice man." Scar gestured to Adam who had a confused look on his face. When he realized he was being talked about he reacted like he had been thinking about something else.

"Huh? Oh, yes. Those are from my garden. Enjoy." Adam smiled at the little girl.

"Thanks." She walked off examining the vegetables.

Scar looked at Adam to gage his reaction to seeing his niece. His face seemed expressionless to Scar. He always had trouble reading white people. They all seemed the same to him.

The kids had been on the news as missing so Scar needed to know if Adam had recognized her. He couldn't just outright ask him. *Shit. What do I do?* Scar thought.

"She came to visit and see my new place. Get her out of the city for a few days." Scar said the first thing that popped in his head.

"Sure. Right. That's what I heard this morning. Fireworks. Funny, I thought it might be gunshots or something. Oh well, I've taken up enough of your time." Adam briskly walked out the front door. Little did Scar know, Adam had come over because he had heard the gunshots and came to investigate. Adam hated guns; they actually scared him.

Scar was shocked. He didn't know what to do. Did Adam recognize his niece? Did he recognize Scar? Why did he seem so strange after his niece came in the house? There were too many unanswered questions for Scars liking. He decided he needed to stop Adam before he alerted the cops. He pulled his gun out of his waistband and went out the front door. The second he got past the threshold he ran right into Flex.

"Ay yo. Where you goin' in such a rush nigga?" Flex said.

"Kill my country ass neighbor."

"Who? That cracker I saw just walk in them woods?"

"Yeah, that him. He already in the woods? Fuck."

Scar thought about chasing him but decided it might be best not to kill him. He figured the dudes wife probably knew where he was going and would come looking for him if he didn't come back. Scar would just have to be on high alert from now on.

"You want me to take care of it boss?" Flex reached for the gun in his coat pocket.

"Nah. Leave it. We just need to be on guard. Matter of fact, get a nigga in here to install a security system. We can see if them mu'fuckin' police tryin' to creep up on us."

"Bet." Flex entered the house.

Scar looked toward the woods before he re-entered the house. *Damn. I thought it would be peaceful up in the country. Nigga can't get away from stress anywhere.*

Chapter 2

Powdered Courage

Security at the former Chief of Staff, Dexter Coram's funeral was tight. The procession of politicians from the city and state seemed endless. Not because they liked Dexter and wanted to pay their respects, but because every press outlet was there and they could get their faces on TV and their names in the papers. In fact, most of them were grossed out by Dexter, if they didn't think they could promote their agendas they wouldn't be there.

Lurking just on the outskirts of the funeral was former Mayor Mathias Steele. The disgraced former mayor was not invited to the funeral. Most of the city was blaming him for the death of Dexter Coram. His tenure as mayor of the city of Baltimore was riddled with corruption. Many people in his government had been killed including three police chiefs and most every member of the drug task force, the DES The only surviving member of the DES was Derek Fuller, who happened to be the brother of the most notorious gangster in Baltimore, Scar Johnson.

Look at these hypocritical sons of bitches Mathias snarled as he watched the politicians enter the church. The park across the street from the church created a nice vantage point for him to watch without being seen or recognized. *Not one of those cocksuckers is clean, and they all turned their backs on me.* Mathias was enraged and mumbling to himself like a homeless person. The minute word got out that the governor was forcing Mathias to step down as mayor, no one would return his phone calls. All of his once-allies were now his enemies and he was hell bent on making them pay for their disloyalty. *You'll get yours you bastards. I'll make sure of it. First I'll take out Scar Johnson and then y'all are next.* He took mental notes of every politician who entered the church.

As the crowd out in front of the church was dwindling and the funeral seemingly about to start, the biggest motorcade of them all came rolling in. From the limousine stepped Governor Thomas Tillingham. Mathias' blood boiled at the sight of the governor. Governor Tillingham was the one man Mathias needed to stand behind him but the governor was the first to turn his back.

Mathias watched the governor shake a few hands and make his presence known before entering the church. The hoopla died down and calm descended upon the street. The only people left were the press and secret service agents keeping an eye on the surrounding area. After calming himself down, Mathias sat on a bench and read the newspaper he had bought on his way to the funeral. His calm didn't last for long. The headline that he had been avoiding since he bought the paper brought his anger right back. It read *How Much Did He Steele?* The following article was full of speculation about Mathias and his time as mayor. Mathias was angry about the article and the things being said about him, but the thing that really upset him was the part of the article that said the Governor had come in and taken over Baltimore. The reporter wrote that officially the Deputy Mayor was in charge but everyone in politics knew that Governor Tillingham had taken control and was cleaning up the corruption left behind by Mathias. Mathias felt like the article made him look incompetent and blamed him for all of the city's problems. Mathias blamed Scar for the problems in the city. *I'm gonna clear my name and show these fuckers who is really responsible for this shit.* Mathias folded the newspaper closed and turned his eyes back to the front of the church. He watched the congregation file out after the funeral service. Governor Tillingham appeared at the top of the steps and the media swarmed. The governor held court like a king among his peasants. Mathias seethed on the inside.

As the governor was speaking to the press he looked across the street into the park. Without missing a beat he whispered into the ear of one of his staff who then whispered into the ear of one of the secret service. The next thing Mathias knew there was a secret service agent standing right next to him.

"Sir, I am going to have to ask you to leave." The agent said to Mathias.

"This is a public park. I think I'll stay." Mathias calmly replied without looking at the agent.

"Sir, I don't want to ask you again. You need to leave this area. It is for security purposes." He said a little more forcefully.

"I am no threat and you can't make me leave a public space. Now I'm asking you to leave."

Mathias replied keeping his eyes locked on Governor Tillingham.

The governor was watching the whole thing transpire as he kept answering questions from the press.

The agent quietly spoke into the microphone attached to the sleeve of his suit then awaited the reply from his superior. "Copy." The agent answered.

"Sir, if you do not cooperate I will have no choice but to use force to remove you."

"Fuck you." Mathias lost his cool. "Do you know who I am? I am the mayor of Baltimore. You take orders from me." Mathias was staring at his reflection in the agents sunglasses.

The agent grabbed Mathias by the arm with one hand, while his other hand was on his weapon. He picked Mathias up off the bench and began shoving him away from the church.

"If you do not leave now I will arrest you."

"Fuck you. I am the mayor!"

"No sir, you were the mayor. Now you are no one." The agent pushed Mathias to the ground.

Mathias was humiliated and wanted to jump up and fight the agent. He thought better of it when he looked up at the agent standing over him with his weapon drawn.

"You'll regret this." Mathias stood up covered in dirt and walked away steaming mad.

It was now a tie between Scar and the governor at the top of Mathias' most hated list. As he walked away Mathias vowed to himself to give a little pay back to the governor for his disrespect.

Mathias walked into East Baltimore with one thing on his mind. He needed to buy a gun. He didn't know how to go about buying a gun but he figured he had a good chance of buying in the 'hood. As mayor he spent no time in these neighborhoods. This was all new territory to him. He felt like an exposed target walking these streets. His attire made him stick out like a sore thumb. He tried to appear calm as he proceeded down Eastern Ave. His eyes were darting back and forth, his body was tense like he was waiting for an attack at any minute.

A young boy about thirteen years old jumped out of a doorway and blocked Mathias' from going any further.

"The fuck you doin' around here nigga?" The boy asked.

"I'm looking to purchase something." Mathias said.

"You got money, I got what you need. I can make you feel good."

"I'm not here to buy drugs."

"The fuck you need then?"

"Young man I doubt you can help me. I need to speak with someone older. Perhaps you have an older brother?"

The young banger looked at Mathias with disgust and confusion on his face. They stood staring at each other. The boy trying to figure this dude out and Mathias not knowing what to do or how these negotiations were supposed to happen.

"Yeah a'ight. I can introduce you to my brother. He inside. Follow me."

They walked toward the boarded up house they were standing in front of. The boy walked up the three steps to the front door and pushed the plywood board back so they could enter. As soon as Mathias was inside the doorway the young boy spun around and caught Mathias with a fist to his jaw sending Mathias slamming into the wall.

"Mu'fucka who you think you is? I got what you need." The boy stood in front of Mathias pointing a gun at him.

Mathias was stunned.

"Now what you need nigga?"

"I, I need a gun." Mathias stammered. His heart was racing. Never in his life had he been in a situation where his life could end any second. He had been sheltered his whole life. He was now getting a taste of what the streets were really like.

"Shit. Why you think I cain't get that for you?"

"I don't know. I've never bought a gun before."

"You a cop?"

"No."

"You look like a cop. I hate cops. I have no problem shooting cops."

"I'm not. I'm not I swear." Mathias was trembling.

The boy stood there studying Mathias. He wasn't nervous at all. He had been on the streets since he was nine. He lost any fear he had years ago.

"Open yo', shirt."

"What?"

"Open yo' shirt. I want to see if y'all wired."

"What?"

The boy reached out and ripped open Mathias shirt exposing his bare chest.

"A'ight, you ain't wired. Step into my home." The boy pushed Mathias deeper inside the house and followed behind keeping his gun aimed at Mathias' back.

The house was dark and cold. There was no furniture except for a television, a dirty mattress on the floor and an old torn up couch in the living room. The boy pushed Mathias down onto the couch. Mathias was beginning to think his life was going to end in this God forsaken place.

The boy pulled a pen cap out of his pocket along with a baggie full of cocaine and tossed both to Mathias.

"Before we go any further in our transaction and for me to feel comfortable with you, you need to take a bump from that baggie."

"I don't know what that means." Mathias caught the baggie and pen cap.

"Nigga snort some cocaine from the bag so I know you legit. Scoop it out with the pen cap and snort it."

"I'm not here to buy drugs."

"Mu'fucka if you don't snort some shit right now, you gonna die." He raised the gun and aimed it a Mathias' head.

"OK, OK." Mathias opened the bag, scooped out a huge bump and snorted it up his left nostril. He immediately felt a burning then numbing sensation in his nostril. To him it felt like the cocaine shot straight through his skull directly into his brain. His eyes widened and his heart started racing. He felt great.

"Wow!" Mathias smiled which made the boy smile as well.

"Now I know you legit. You want a gun? You wanna be a gangbanger grandpa?"

"Yeah I need a gun." The cocaine was making Mathias clench his jaw.

"A'ight. I can get you a gun. But you ain't just buying a gun from me. I'm a businessman and my business is cocaine. You need to buy some shit from me so my bosses can see I'm hustlin' out here."

"Oh, definitely. Whatever you need." Mathias' leg was twitching rapid fire.

"How much money you got?"

"I have a thousand dollars. Is that enough?"

The boy didn't say anything. He just stared at Mathias. This was much more than the boy was going to ask for. He didn't say anything because he was trying to hide his shock and excitement.

"Damn. That's all you have? Usually I wouldn't do this, but I like you so I'll sell you a gun and that bag for a thousand. You gettin' a good deal. Normally it would be at least fifteen hundred."

"Thanks I appreciate it." Thoughts were racing through Mathias' mind a mile a minute. He reached in his pocket and handed the boy the stack of cash.

"Bullets not included." The boy emptied the clip of his gun and handed it to Mathias.

"Oh sure, yeah, of course." Mathias put the gun in his pocket. Now that their transaction was complete both of them couldn't wait to leave. The boy wanted to jet before this dude realized he got suckered. Mathias wanted to leave because the cocaine had him so high he needed to get outside and walk.

"You need more coke, you come see me. I got rock too if you need it."

"Yeah, yeah, OK." Mathias walked out as fast as he could.

Once on the street Mathias was so high he didn't realize that he speed walked all the way back to his nice safe section of Baltimore. The cocaine had him flying high and feeling like he could conquer the world. He was positive that he would destroy Scar and Governor Tillingham now that he had a gun. He felt invincible and couldn't wait to get home to do another bump of coke.